RIVERDALE

GET OUT OF TOWN

An original novel by Micol Ostow

SCHOLASTIC INC.

Copyright © 2019 by Archie Comic Publications, Inc.

All rights reserved. Published by Scholastic Inc., *Publishers since 1920*. SCHOLASTIC and associated logos are trademarks and/or registered trademarks of Scholastic Inc.

The publisher does not have any control over and does not assume any responsibility for author or third-party websites or their content.

No part of this publication may be reproduced, stored in a retrieval system, or transmitted in any form or by any means, electronic, mechanical, photocopying, recording, or otherwise, without written permission of the publisher. For information regarding permission, write to Scholastic Inc., Attention: Permissions Department, 557 Broadway, New York, NY 10012.

This book is a work of fiction. Names, characters, places, and incidents are either the product of the author's imagination or are used fictitiously, and any resemblance to actual persons, living or dead, business establishments, events, or locales is entirely coincidental.

ISBN 978-1-338-28948-0

10 9 8 7 6 5 4 3 2 1   19 20 21 22 23

Printed in the U.S.A. 23

First printing 2019

Book design by Jessica Meltzer

PART ONE: THE PARTY

PROLOGUE

JUGHEAD

Summer. Just the mention of the word conjures a series of comforting images. Long evenings spent watching the sunset creep over the horizon, fireflies lighting up the air like renegade Fourth of July sparklers. Lazy days on a porch swing nursing a soft-serve cone, trying to strike the balance between savoring the treat and devouring it before it liquefies, sticky-sweet, under the searing press of the sun's glow.

Summer is for being idle, for swatting mosquitos and splashing in Sweetwater River, for ignoring the alarm clock and losing track of time. It's for living in that state of suspended animation where any semblance of responsibility evaporates and it's just you, your best friends, and the sensation that everything you do and are is ephemeral, hazy . . . and yours alone.

In Riverdale, summer belongs to us.

Or that's what we thought, anyway. Until *this* summer. Until Archie Andrews was arrested for murder and forced to spend the summer before his junior year standing trial. Before we were forced to consider the terrifying—and terrifyingly real—possibility that Archie's trial was only the beginning.

Cassidy Bullock. We weren't necessarily torn up about his death. After all, he and his thug friends *had* terrorized us when we were up at Veronica's cabin in Shadow Lake for the weekend. And they probably would have done worse if Veronica hadn't triggered the silent alarm.

So we weren't sorry he'd been killed (presumably by the Lodge family bodyguard, Andre). What we *were* sorry about was that Hiram Lodge, Veronica's father, had framed Archie for the murder. And that the charges had stuck.

Endless summer. Summer love. The poet Wallace Stevens wrote that "summer night is like a perfection of thought." But for Archie, Veronica, Betty, and me, there was no perfection to be found. Only the relentlessness of reality.

For Archie, that reality meant reviewing his testimony until he was as familiar with it as he was with breathing. It was examining the case Hiram Lodge had built against him with a proverbial fine-tooth comb, alongside his mother, Mary Andrews, arguably the most devoted counsel a teen accused of murder could have in his corner.

Second to Mary on the Team Archie lineup was Betty Cooper, pragmatic and determined as always. Last summer, the sunny-with-a-side-of-edge girl next door was brushing up on her journalistic skills with an internship at a lifestyle blog in LA. Now, though, she was using her investigative talents to prove that her oldest friend's innocence. All this on the heels of finding out that her father was the serial killer Riverdale had known as the Black Hood.

Meanwhile, Riverdale's resident fish out of water, Veronica Lodge, had rejected her sizable birthright—and the tarnished strings that came with it. The one-time princess of Park Avenue had turned her back on her family name and all the financial security that it implied. And while she was trying to stake a claim of her own as the newest owner of Pop's Chock'Lit Shoppe, she was *also* horn-locked—and hopelessly deadlocked—with Daddy Dearest. The price at the heart of their feverish feud?

One Archie Andrews's liberty. Maybe even his soul.

As for me, I was doing my best to honor my own father's sense of loyalty, of family, adapting to my new role as Serpent King. I was worried for Archie, of course—more like desperately scared for him—though I was trying to keep a positive spin on things. (It doesn't come easy to me, to say the least.) But I had a gang—literally—looking to me, depending on me to lead them. The Serpents would have done anything for me, and for the Andrewses, too, especially after they put us up when Hiram Lodge displaced anyone unlucky enough to be living on the Southside. With my dad retired from the Serpents, it was time for me to show people I deserved their trust and faith.

The problem was, I wasn't sure I believed it.

When Jason Blossom was murdered, the town of Riverdale lost something innate, something ineffable. For decades, our tiny community shimmered with wholesome, small-town charm. No one bothered to peel back the facade, to strip away the picture-perfect Norman Rockwell homage. No one wanted to . . . Not even those who knew better. Those who knew all too well this town's secrets, and its rotting, dark-hearted core.

Jason Blossom. The Black Hood. And now Archie Andrews, one-time small-town golden boy, on trial for murder, twisting under a disgraced mobster's thumb. Poised to lose everything for the simple mistake of crossing the wrong man.

Summer had stretched, sticky and unforgiving, tangling the four of us in an intricate web. The days were endless, like all summer days, but now the heavy molasses pace felt dangerous, threatening.

Labor Day was bearing down. Most teens would be dreading going back to school: homework, cliques, early wake-ups.

We weren't thinking about that. We would have given anything to be thinking about stuff like that. Instead, we were worried that Archie's last chance—his last shot at freedom, at beating Hiram Lodge at his own game—was slipping away from us.

And if we couldn't save Archie from the dark horrors lying at Riverdale's heart, who would?

CHAPTER ONE

Reggie:

Party at Casa Mantle tonight, bro.

Archie:

Not sure I'm in a partying mood, man. Sorry.

Reggie:

I hear you. But my folks are out of town, and you've got closing arguments next week, yeah?

Archie:

Don't remind me.

Reggie:

What else can you do? Your mom has def got this covered. Take a night to just chill. You could prob use it, right?

Archie:

Don't want to leave my mom alone while she's busting her ass for me.

Reggie:

She's your MOM. Guarantee she wants you to have one night of being a normal guy and not an accused murderer.

Reggie:

Tell me I'm wrong.

Archie:

. . .

Reggie:

I'm gonna round up the rest of the Bulldogs. Then I'm texting Veronica. Between her and your mom, I'll count on you being here.

Reggie:

One night off. Then you can go back to Dead Man Walking.

Archie:

Gee, thanks.

Reggie:

JK, dude. You're gonna be cleared. Put it out of your mind. Just for tonight.

Archie:

Will try. Easier said than done.

Reggie:

What isn't, man? 👊

∧∧∧

Veronica:

Archiekins, I just got the most interesting text from Reggie Mantle . . . ✳🎂 🍷🍷

Archie:

Ronnie, ILU, but are you sure a party is the best idea? Even if I were in the mood—we should be working. On my case. Or, I should be. Mom WILL be.

Veronica:

All work and no play makes Archie a dull boy. Don't you remember your King-by-way-of-Kubrick?

Archie:

If it's not from Carrie: The Musical, I haven't read it yet.

Veronica:

Kidding, dearie. But anyway, you deserve some fun.

Archie:

. . . Because it may be the last fun I see in a while, you mean.

Veronica:

I didn't say that. And I refuse to entertain negative energy. I have 100% faith in our ability to prove your innocence. BUT I still think we deserve a night off.

Archie:

But my mom . . .

Veronica:

Not to worry. Your mom thinks it's a fabulous idea, of course. She was thrilled when I suggested it.

Archie:

What about Betty?

Veronica:

She was harder to convince, babbling about files and highlighters, that girl is the true definition of ride-or-die, but your mom talked her into it. Proof that you really do have the most persuasive lawyer. And can take. One night. To breathe.

Archie:

What are the chances I'm gonna talk you out of this?

Veronica:

About the same as your chances of being convicted for a crime you didn't commit.

Veronica:

In other words, I'll pick you up at 8.

ᴧᴧᴧ

Veronica:

Archie's in, of course.

Betty:

Your powers of persuasion, V. A+. ✋

Veronica:

Never underestimate a Lodge's determination.

Betty:

Ugh. Don't remind me. That's just what I'm afraid of . . .

Veronica:

Nope! Cease and desist, sister. Forget I said anything. Good vibes only tonight. See you soon!

∧∧∧

Betty:

Dust off your dutiful boyfriend hat, Jug.

Jughead:

I only have the one hat, Betty. You know that. Anyway, I heard. Party at Reggie's. I've had anxiety dreams more pleasant than the prospect.

Betty:

You're doing it for Archie. And me. ☺

Jughead:

I can't say this is my most festive hour. I don't even HAVE a most festive hour. But I can't say no to you, either.

Betty:

> XOXO

∧∧∧

Cheryl:

> JoJo! LA is such a delight. I'm so glad Toni talked me into this cross-country jaunt! We're like . . . Thelma and Louise, but without the tragic ending, of course. And if Susan Sarandon was a genuine ginger, like moi. Have you been following on insta? #ChoniGoesWest.

Josie:

> Girl, you know I'm following your excellent adventures. And I'm glad you're having fun. The cats are hanging in by our sharp little claws. Riverdale is same old, same old, small-time small-town.

Cheryl:

> How many times do I have to tell you, you're too good for the town that time forgot? You should be in La La Land with us!

Cheryl:

> Last night we saw a show at Tom Sawyer & tonight we're doing Hotel Cafe. Toni has a Serpent hookup basically everywhere that's anywhere. It's the ultimate VIP pass.

Cheryl:

The next road trip will be a Pussycats tour.
I volunteer as booking agent.

Josie:

Good looking out, Bombshell. Meanwhile I'm
getting text-bombed by Reggie Mantle about a
house party tonight. Not exactly bright lights, big
city. When you get back, you can work my security
detail, too. Mantle wouldn't stand a chance.

Cheryl:

Men are such dogs. And that boy is a dog with
a bone. So are you going?

Josie:

Not sure. Gotta check in with my kitties.
Maybe one of them has a better offer.

Cheryl:

Well, hope springs eternal, Josephine. Crossing
my cherry-cosmo-lacquered fingers for you.
Keep me posted!

∧∧∧

Kevin:

Party at Reggie's tonight. You there?

Moose:

Yeah, man. I'll find you there, OK?

Kevin:

I thought maybe we could go together?

Moose:

. . .

Kevin:

Never mind. I'll just see you there. TTYL.

∧∧∧

VERONICA

Normally, a house party hosted by a small-town jock isn't the sort of event that I'd rush to add to the top of my social calendar. But that was before I lost my heart to a small-town jock myself . . . and then watched in abject horror as my increasingly cartoon-villain-evil father corrupted my beloved paramour and ultimately threatened to put him behind bars.

It makes a girl anxious. Understandably. This summer, I was reevaluating a lot of my previously held tenets.

Mind you, I was thoroughly certain that the mere truth of Archie's innocence would exonerate him. And if anyone could bring justice to light, it was Mrs. Andrews and Betty. Hell hath no fury—and no drive—like those two.

But *certain* is a relative term . . . And, while it's one I use unwaveringly in the presence of Archie and our friends, the whole unvarnished truth was—is always—a little stickier.

I know my father. Maybe not *quite* as well as I'd always thought—for starters, I never thought he'd stoop so low as to actually frame the love of my life for any crime, let alone *murder*. I knew when Archie started getting closer to my father that there was danger my all-American boy would be corrupted. In fact, I warned Archie of just that. But a part of me wanted to believe that even Hiram Lodge had ethical limits.

Clearly, I was wrong. It turns out Daddy doesn't have a rock bottom.

And if I was so wrong about that, then who's to say I wasn't also wrong about Archie's chances at an acquittal?

These were the thoughts that were keeping me up at night, tossing and turning in my 1,800-thread-count Frette sheets.

Veronica Lodge is nothing if not unflappable. That's basically my personal brand. And that was the image I was going to project for my friends, for our town, for as long as it took to clear Archie's name. Like a country song cliché, I'd stand by my man. Even if my legs were feeling a little shaky.

The thing about having a monster for a father is this: People have sympathy. Sure, some of those people are indebted to Daddy and need to make sure their *i*'s are dotted and their *t*'s are crossed. I can't blame them. *Some* people—the less valiant of the populace—would never visibly go against my father. It didn't take long—after my father revealed his true visage, after our family's fall from grace—for me to sort the cowards out of my contacts list. Now I know who I can count on.

Since we lost Andre, I've had the household staff wrapped around my finger. Our new driver is basically my bestie. Which meant he was all too happy to drive Archie and me to Reggie's house for a brief respite from the courtroom drama that had haunted us all summer long. Luckily, Daddy had a late-night "business" call (no doubt shady AF)—meaning that he was locked in his office at the Pembrooke. Even if we weren't engaged in the domestic version of a cold war, he wouldn't have noticed my departure.

I suppose there are occasional upsides to having a complete Fascist for a father.

The sun had already set by the time we pulled up to the Mantle abode, just another reminder that summer days were waning, and fast. Fall was just around the corner, and with it, the threat that school would start and regular life in

Riverdale would resume, everything reverting to normal, as it does, every year. Only this time, all that might happen without Archie. I shivered, and not just because of the chill in the air.

"Miss Veronica, we're here. Unless there's something else you require."

The driver's gruff voice broke through the chaos in my head. I cleared my throat delicately, smoothing the sharp pleats of the skirt of my Kate Spade minidress. It was a vibrant purple print, more festive than I felt on the inside. That was the whole point. *Fake it till you make it*, a mantra that had proven helpful in trying times.

Archie put a warm hand over mine. "Everything okay, Ronnie?" I could feel the calloused pads of his fingers where he'd worn them down practicing guitar. I knew those hands like they were part of my own body. The thought that I might lose Archie?

It was unbearable. I *had* to fake it better. For Archie's sake.

I forced a smile. "Everything's great!" My voice sounded too high in my ears. I blinked and waved a hand in the direction of the front door. "Looks like we're fashionably late. Perfect."

The party was clearly in full swing, deep bass thrumming even all the way inside our car and a crush of bodies moving frenetically against the living room picture window. I could hear chatter outside, floating toward us from around the backyard. The garage door was open and a bunch of boys from the football team hovered inside, surrounded by a cluster of adoring River Vixens.

I leaned to Archie and gave him a quick kiss on the cheek. "Let's make an entrance, Archiekins."

~~~

PP:

Are you in? Look around for poss. partners. We need a reliable Riverdale in, the Big Man is counting on it.

Sweet Pea:

Relax. Haven't left yet. And not sure I want to be your inside guy on this. I've got other plans for the party.

PP:

That's cute. Too bad you have no say in the matter.

CHAPTER TWO

Josie:

My kitties. I know the Pussycats are on a . . . hiatus. But seeing as we have our one-night-only headline against our rivals, Venom . . .

Josie:

Maybe a little pre-show bonding is in order? Like the good old days?

Melody:

What did you have in mind?

Josie:

Maybe a drive-by for Mantle's party?

Valerie:

You serious? Feels a little B-list as far as blowing off steam goes.

Josie:

Yeah, but he's been blowing up my phone all morning. Resistance is futile?

Josie:

Come on . . . For old times' sake?

Valerie:

I don't know, girlfriend . . .

Melody:

I mean, Riverdale High = the cornerstone of our fan base. We might as well make an appearance. We can move on to bigger and better after.

Josie:

Exactly. Just a drive-by. Pick you up 8-ish. Let's get in, get out, and get on with our night.

∿∿∿

Josie:

Settled: We'll be at Reggie's after 8. But we aren't gonna linger.

Sweet Pea:

See you there.

Josie:

Remember: LOW-KEY, or this is over.

Sweet Pea:

^^^

ARCHIE

When Veronica told me she wanted to go to Reggie's party, my first impulse was *no way*. Even if Mom weren't sweating my legal case 24/7—with Betty always by her side—being the defendant in a murder trial doesn't exactly put a guy in the partying mood.

But of course, as much as Ronnie may despise her father, she does have one major thing in common with him: My girl does *not* take no for an answer. Veronica Lodge gets what she wants. And what she wanted tonight was one night off from all the stress and drama *I* brought into her life. She warned me, way back when, that getting involved with Hiram was a bad idea. I thought she was just being dramatic, overprotective. God, I was so naïve. And the ironic thing? The only reason I ever wanted to win Hiram over in the first place was because he's Veronica's father.

Veronica's dad may be evil, but *I'm* the one who made bad, stupid choices and got myself into this whole mess. Now I'm watching the stress and pain I'm putting my parents through, seeing my friends completely freaked out . . . I just wish more than anything I could take it all back.

And since life doesn't work that way, the next best thing I have to offer—the *only* thing I have, right now—is to give Ronnie (and the rest of them) one "normal" night.

"Let's make an entrance, Archiekins." Veronica kissed me quickly on the cheek, and I could smell that thick rush of roses and whatever else dark and musky goes into the expensive perfume she always wears. She was putting on a brave face for me, I could tell—that girl is *fierce*—but I could feel the waves of tension radiating off her, like heat or static electricity. *I'd* done that. It was my fault, how upset she was.

I thanked the driver and got out of the car, walking around to let Ronnie out in an old-fashioned, gentlemanly way. She smiled and held out a hand as she stepped out.

"Chivalry is not dead," she quipped. "Promise me you'll always be my knight in shining armor."

"Count on it," I said. We were doing our best to be light, but the weight of my trial hanging over us put a damper on everything.

"Andrews!" I looked up. It was Chuck Clayton, waving a plastic cup at me like he was cheers-ing from a distance.

"Yo!" I gave my best smile and a noncommittal grunt. Chuck wasn't anyone's favorite since he'd spread nasty rumors after going on a date with Ronnie when she first got to town. That was bad enough, but when Betty and Ronnie decided to get revenge on him, they discovered that a bunch of guys from the football team had this whole sick "points" system where they tracked their hookups with girls. They literally had a notebook where they kept score of everything they did. When the girls took the notebook to Principal Weatherbee, Chuck and a few others were suspended from the team.

So as you might guess, there was no love lost between Chuck Clayton and Veronica, and I didn't blame her for holding a grudge. He wasn't my favorite guy, either, though since being suspended, he seemed genuinely sorry about everything.

Veronica glanced in Chuck's direction. She wrinkled her nose for a second, but then that smile was back. "You should go say hi. I mean, even if he was kicked off the Bulldogs, you guys were teammates."

"You don't need that. You brought me here so we could have *fun*."

"Don't you get it, Archiekins? I'm here with you. Ergo, I'm having fun." Veronica's dark eyes glittered. "*You* are all I need." She gave me a little shove. "Go, say hi, be the dutiful alpha male I know and adore. I'll meet you inside. I want to see if Betty and Jughead are here yet."

I opened my mouth to say something, but she tapped me again, playful. "Seriously, Archie. Veronica Lodge can take care of herself at a party. You know that."

"I do." We kissed again, quickly, and she disappeared up the walk and into the front door. The roar of amped-up high schoolers swelled and then dulled as the door opened and shut behind her.

I made my way to the garage. It was wall-to-wall Riverdale High. Through the crowd, I could see a cooler, and in the corner, a keg—probably someone on the block would call the cops sooner rather than later. In Riverdale, parents tend to turn a blind eye when kids get rowdy, blowing off steam, but this thing was *loud*, and it was just getting started.

There was Chuck, and Moose . . . and against the wall, eyeing the cooler suspiciously, I saw Kevin Keller. His father was the former sheriff of Riverdale. But he'd had to step down after the Black Hood killed Midge. As Sheriff Keller's son, Kevin probably got used to turning a blind eye at, um, "after-school events." And I'm guessing old habits died hard. I felt a little bad for him. It had to be rough, always feeling torn between what your dad expected of you and what all the other kids were doing.

I had plenty of experience with falling short of other people's expectations.

"Hey, Archie!" Kevin brightened, seeing me. "Welcome to the den of iniquity. Where's Veronica?"

"She went inside," I explained, shouting to be heard over all the conversation. "Didn't want to . . ." I trailed off when Chuck sidled up next to me. *Awkward.*

"Didn't want to . . . what? Have to associate with low-level pervs like me?" he asked, laughing loudly at his own "joke."

"Come on, Chuck." I rolled my eyes. "Give her a break." The last thing I needed or wanted was to argue with my friends. Not if this might be one of the last times we all hung out.

He shrugged. "For you, Andrews. Not for her. The Clayton memory is long."

I didn't care who he did it for, as long as he dropped it so we could all relax. Someone shoved a red plastic cup in my hand and, without thinking about it, I took a big gulp. It was sour and cold and tasted like the promise of oblivion. Right then, those all sounded like good things. Another good thing? Chuck disappeared, trailing after a curly brown-haired ponytail in a River Vixens uniform.

"You been here long?" I asked, turning back to Kevin. His eyes darted around the space, like he was nervous about something, although when he heard my question, he gave me a strained smile.

What was it with everyone being on edge tonight? I thought it was just me, with the stress of the trial, but honestly, it kind of felt like everyone was off their game.

"Uh, a little while, I guess. I was trying to play it cool, make an entrance, but it didn't end up working out that way," he said, sheepish. "Don't tell Veronica, she won't approve. I officially have no chill."

"Your secret's safe with me," I assured him. "I lost my chill a while back. Who's here?"

"You mean, aside from basically the entire junior and senior classes? I think it would probably be more efficient to list the kids who *aren't* here tonight." He tried to gesture to the bodies stuffed into the space around us, but he didn't have enough room to spread his arms out. Which kind of proved his point. "Betty's inside; she and Jughead got here right before you did. I just got to talk to her for a second before she ran off. She seemed . . . Well, she seemed a little jittery, to be honest. So you know, I mean. If you talk to her later. Maybe just keep an eye out. I'm rambling." He tilted his head toward a corner. "Moose is over there. With a *Vixen*." His face crumpled.

I didn't have a chance to ask him about it, though—the face, or what he was saying (or trying to say) about Betty. Next thing I knew, he was stepping back and making room for Reggie.

"Our gracious host himself!" Kevin said. "Reggie, this is quite a turnout. Kudos."

"Thanks, man. Yeah. I guess Dad always traveling has its perks. And since Mom decided it was time to treat herself to another spa getaway, it's just Vader and me—two alpha dogs. Lone wolves, together."

"Wouldn't a *lone wolf* necessarily be, you know . . . *alone*?" Kevin asked.

Reggie rolled his eyes. "You know what I mean."

Reggie's dad owned a car dealership in town. It was really successful; Reggie wasn't rich the way that Veronica was (well, the way her parents were, since technically she'd decided to emancipate herself from them)—but his house was in the nicest part of town, with bigger lawns and shinier cars in the driveways. I wasn't sure why a car dealer had to travel so much, but it wasn't the kind of thing I could ask Reggie about.

"Don't you get lonely?" I blurted. *Speaking of things you're not supposed to ask about.* It was a weird thing to say, definitely not the kind of question we usually asked each other. But it was out of my mouth before I thought about it. And then there was no taking it back.

Reggie's face got dark for a minute. But after a second, he smiled and his expression went back to normal. "Andrews," he said, leaning in so Kevin and I could hear him. "Look around you, man. This house is *packed*. Who'd be lonely in this?"

I nodded, even though it felt kind of like he was missing my point. If that was on purpose, well, then, whatever. Sometimes a little denial can go a long way. I was learning that myself.

"Duh," I said, shaking my head. "Sorry."

He clapped me on the shoulder. "Whatever, bro. I get it. You've got deep thoughts on the brain."

"Is it that obvious?" I flushed and took another gulp of my drink. *Slow down, Archie,* I told myself. But slowing down meant letting those so-called "deep thoughts" rise up, and I didn't think I could handle that.

"I mean, I would, too, if I were in your shoes," Reggie said. Kevin nodded. "This is big-time. *Murder.*"

Thanks, I'd almost gone four whole minutes without thinking about it. I had to bite my tongue to keep from snapping. Instead I took another sip. "Yeah."

"I'm sure Archie is all too aware of how 'big-time' the *murder trial* is," Kevin said. "What with the murder part of it. Maybe we could try to forget about it, just for the night?"

"Yeah, what he said," I agreed. "If we can." I wasn't sure about that—like I said, the energy coming off people was weird. Even Reggie seemed off, like he was itching for a fight. But maybe it was just me. It was probably me. It was a bad idea, coming to this party tonight.

It all came down to Veronica. She was the reason I was in this mess in the first place—not that I *blamed* her, at all! But I wouldn't be out even pretending to have fun if it weren't what she wanted. "That was Ronnie's whole thing," I went on, kind of thinking out loud. "You know, to come out, have fun, take our mind off things. It's, uh, not easy."

Reggie gave me a look. I already knew I wouldn't like where this was going. "This must be hard on her, too. Knowing it's her old man getting you sent away."

Kevin arched an eyebrow. "I mean, understatement of the century, much? When your father is a crime boss with half of Riverdale's underbelly in his back pocket, hell-bent on destroying everything you love—including your high school sweetheart? Yeah, I think it makes a girl shy."

"Yeah, well—" Reggie took a big gulp from his red cup. "That's one thing you won't have to worry about, Andrews. If they lock you up, I mean."

"What?" His words hit me like a punch to the stomach. *You don't have to worry about your girl.* Was he saying what I thought he was saying? Because that was low. Even for the cocky, aggressive Reggie I used to know.

"What?" Kevin said at the same time. He looked as surprised as I felt.

"Come on, I'm not saying, like, they're going to lock you up *for sure.* Just, you know, *if* they do. Put you away." He stumbled a little while my stomach twisted. "You should know Veronica . . . *Ronnie* . . . will be looked after." He winked. "By me."

My face went hot and I stood up straighter, throwing back my shoulders and getting ready to launch myself at Reggie. A sheet of red swam before my eyes. Kevin held an arm out to keep me back.

"Easy there, Rocky," he warned. "The last thing you need is *another* incident added to your history of violence."

Reggie held his hands up in a "who, me?" gesture. His drink sloshed over the rim of his cup, dousing his shirt. "Crap!"

Kevin's hand tightened around my wrist. "Come on, let's save the fight club stuff for later," he said, pulling me through the crowd and out of the garage. "Reggie Mantle is *not* worth it. Also, he's had, like, five of those drinks, so I wouldn't take anything he says seriously. Or personally."

"Easy for you to say," I mumbled.

"Is it, though?" Kevin sighed. "That was a bonehead thing to say. But, you know—Reggie's a bonehead. And he's even more of a jerk when he's been drinking. The good news is, Veronica Lodge is immune to boneheads and jerks. Not to mention totally in love with you. So no matter how oafish Reggie is being—now or in the unfathomable event of the worst-case scenario outcome—you *definitely*, totally, do not have anything to worry about." He paused. "Also, you know Reggie's sensitive about his dad. Calls him *Mein Führer*, and that's one of the nicer nicknames he has. So maybe he was feeling triggered."

"Great. So it's my job to handle Reggie Mantle with kid gloves while *I'm* the one on trial for murder?"

Kevin shrugged. "I mean, no. Of course not. You shouldn't have to give a second thought to Reggie Mantle's state of mind. It's just . . ." he stopped himself.

"It's just, *what*?"

Kevin sighed and gave me a meaningful look. "It's just . . . you're *Archie*."

"What does that even mean?"

"Archie Andrews. You're a 'good guy.' Thinking about Reggie's—about everyone's—state of mind? It's what you do. Even in the middle of a personal crisis. You can't help yourself."

It was my turn to sigh. I took another sip from my drink. It burned going down. Maybe Kevin had a point. Maybe that was my thing: being concerned, being the good guy, the all-American boy next door. But if that was true . . .

How had I ended up *here*?

Where did it all go so wrong?

And how the hell was I going to fix it?

CHAPTER THREE

REGGIE

So, was it cruel to dog my man Archie about his trial and how he might be getting locked up, like, who knows for how long?

Yeah, okay. It wasn't the coolest thing I've ever done. (And maybe I even regret it a little.) But it wasn't the *worst thing*, either. But real talk: Dude kinda deserved to be taken down a peg. Making that random crack about my dad always being on the road? Yeah, I get it—he's a car dealer, why can't he be home and *deal*? But we can't all have perfect TV-sitcom father-son bonds like Fred and Archie Andrews.

(Although, considering how Mary Andrews left those guys, it's pretty clear things were never as picture-perfect as they all like to pretend . . .)

I know I have a rep for being cocky, a little too aggro, but as captain of the Bulldogs, I just think of that as "leadership." You don't get to the top by rolling over and playing nice. And it's not like I had the best example of how to be well-adjusted growing up.

My beef with Andrews goes way back. As far back as Little League, when it was the Mantle versus Little Archie for pitcher. Was I competitive, even back then? Hells yeah. Blame it on Dad. I don't know; Archie and I'd known each other since preschool, Riverdale's a small town, after all, and something about us both being really into sports, real guys' guys, even then, meant that people were always comparing us. But, like, from where I sat, Archie got nothing but approval from his dad. "Be yourself, Arch," Fred would say. "You got this!" he'd call from the bleachers at our practices.

While *my* dad would videotape all our games. (Keep in mind, this was when phone cameras were still pretty janky, so you know he was going the extra mile for this. And I don't mean that like it's a good thing.) He'd scream his head off at the umpire any time I was called out. I wanted to just disappear; it was so humiliating.

But it was worse when we got home. Because *that* was when the real torture would start. He'd bust out the tape and point out all my fumbles and errors, every little false move. He said it would help me "improve my form," "perfect my game." And that was the best-case scenario. Mom would frown in the background, clucking disapproval while she cooked dinner. But she never went so far as to actually say anything. She *definitely* never intervened.

Perfect TV-sitcom was Archie's world, not mine. That was obvious pretty early.

So it should be equally obvious why I can't help but think of him as my number-one competition, all the time. In all arenas.

Giving him hell about Ronnie? Implying that I was gonna make a move on his girl while he's locked away? Okay, kind of harsh. And I'd never really stab my boy in the back like that. But Archie does *fine* with the ladies; he doesn't have to worry. And everyone knows Veronica has total heart-eyes emoji for him, anyway.

That's not to say I couldn't pry her away if I really wanted to—my powers of persuasion are the stuff of legend—but I've got my sights set higher.

Veronica Lodge may be Riverdale's answer to a socialite. But for Reggie Mantle, only a *true* celebrity will do.

A celebrity like Josie McCoy. Talk about your bad kitty.

Problem is, girl's playing hard to get. Like, *extra* hard to get. Like, if I weren't me, I might even wonder if she was really playing.

But of course she is. Because—I *am* me. Truth.

Reggie Mantle may play the field—what can I say, I'm an athlete, yo—but my dirty secret is this: I've had it bad for Josie since forever. I know if she'd just give it a chance, we'd be perfect together. And she's the only one I'd ever tame my ways for.

TBH, the reason I threw this party in the first place was because I was hoping she would come, and I'd maybe get some one-on-one time with her. Maybe it's lame. (But romantic, am I right?) I mean, Archie had a point, the house can be a little empty, even when the rents are both in town. I definitely prefer to have my buds around and stuff. But I could tolerate empty if it weren't for wanting to take a shot with Josie.

Another shot, I mean.

The thing is, I know Josie wants me. If you're paying attention, it's obvious. Even though, like I say, she plays hard to get, she always gives me *just enough* to know that the girl definitely has feelings. So why is she taking her sweet time with this? I guess some people just like the chase, the anticipation.

(And to be fair, she's not wrong—the chase is totally hot.)

I'm all about looking forward, moving forward. Because when I think about some of my past encounters with Josie . . . Well, even when I've gotten the girl, it always fell apart. My rep as a prankster . . . it has its pros, but it also definitely has its cons.

But why dwell? Stuff happens, the past is the past. The only thing anyone needs to know about those past experiences is that through them all, Josie showed me without a doubt that somewhere, on some level, she for sure digs me. That's all the encouragement I need.

She said she'd swing by tonight. Even with a gig tomorrow, so—think about that for a minute. She *wants* to come by.

She wants to see me.

She wants *me*.

Can you blame her?

$\sim\!\sim\!\sim$

BETTY

Dear Diary:

Riverdale is my home, and I love it—even with all the insane, terrible, terrifying things that have happened to me, my friends, my family… everyone who lives here. Maybe I'm just naïve, maybe I'm too hopeful, too "sunny, girl next door" (ugh, I hate that phrase)…but I can't help it. Riverdale is <u>me</u>. It's in my blood.

Of course, there are other things in my blood, too. Like the fact that I share it—I share actual, physical chemistry, DNA—with the Black Hood.

That my father is a serial killer.

That I have my own secrets, too. Darker than a Louise Brooks bob, and way more twisted.

So sue me for wanting to have one fun, normal night with my friends. One night to pretend everything is fine and Veronica's father isn't some mustache-twirling cartoon bad guy. That Archie might not be in real danger of going to prison, despite being the most pure-hearted guy I've ever known. One night of not thinking about my boyfriend's gang affiliations and how I'm his newly minted "Serpent Queen," and what being named Southside royalty means in light of the fact that the Southside isn't even ours anymore.

You get it, right? Why I'd want to pretend? To sweep things under the rug just for a few hours, tops, slap on some lip gloss and paste on a smile? Of course you do.

But this is <u>Riverdale,</u> after all. Nothing can ever be normal.

At least Jug was in a decent mood. I know parties aren't exactly his scene (understatement, to say the least). But when Veronica and I approached him about taking Archie out, he could see right away it would be a good thing for our friend. And who knows how many "good things" Archie has left to look forward to? And for how long.

Mom was being crazy. (What else is new?) You would think that having Polly and the twins home and getting all super obsessed with that creepy farm and Edgar Evernever (<u>really?</u>) would keep her preoccupied. But Alice Cooper is a world-class multitasker. She can totally redesign her entire personality and lifestyle to revolve around this new-age shaman charlatan and still find time to harass her younger daughter. The one who dares to point out Emperor Evernever's OBVIOUS lack of new clothes.

I was in my room wrapping the edges of my ponytail around a curling wand, careful to keep my fingers from sizzling, when she popped into my doorway. "Elizabeth Cooper! Just where do you think you're going, young lady?"

"Young lady." That's when I knew it was going to be good. Or—bad, I guess. Escape was going to be harder than I'd hoped.

I tried to act like I wasn't worried, like her presence wasn't stressing me out at all, even though my veins were humming like there was electricity coursing through them and I had to bite my lip to keep from screaming at the top of my lungs.

Keep it under control, Betty, I told myself. That's the only way to outmaneuver her. That was a lesson I'd learned a million times over by now. I set the curling wand down and spritzed my hair with setting spray. It coated the room in the scent of lilacs, thick and cloying. I tried not to cough.

"Out, Mom," I said, calm. "To Reggie's. He's having a thing."

"A 'thing.' You mean a party. Unchaperoned?"

I rolled my eyes. "His parents are out of town, yes. But come on. It's just Riverdale High kids."

She snorted. "'Just' Riverdale High kids? I suppose Archie will be there. You know I don't approve of him. Or maybe Riverdale High kids like Jason Blossom, who tore your sister's heart out?"

I slammed my hand down on my vanity. So much for calm. The curling wand jumped and sizzled, singeing the wood. Crap. I turned it off. "Mom! Leave it alone. <u>Jason's dead.</u> Polly lost the love of her life—the twins' <u>father.</u> Our family's stupid vendetta against the Blossoms is so pointless. All it did was drive Dad to commit unspeakable acts in the name of some vague morality purge. We need to let it go."

"You're one to talk about letting things go," Mom said, her eyes flashing. "If you'd practice what you preach, you'd be so much healthier."

I sighed and reached for my mascara. "What the hell are you even talking about?"

"You're repressing everything you feel about your father, Elizabeth. You're the one who hasn't even visited him—"

"—I went," I interjected, shuddering at the memory. Looking into my father's cold green eyes, so similar to my own. It was chilling. Jail hadn't made him remorseful. I don't think it even made him human. I told him, "No more darkness." But he didn't flinch, didn't blink. He told me he and I are alike.

In my nightmares, I wonder. I worry that he's right.

Sometimes the pills are the only thing that can keep those thoughts away. The funny thing is, last year, Mom was the one pushing Adderall on me in the first place. I would just pretend to take the pills. And now, I'm lying to her about seeing a shrink and forging my own prescriptions. What a difference a year makes.

And even though the last thing I want is more secrets, I can't let my friends know. About any of it.

"You went once. You need to process, to deal with your feelings. Edgar says—"

"Spare me the Edgar talk, okay?" I shouted, loud enough that she actually shrunk back for a second. "Just because you and Polly have been dragged into a cult—let's just call it what it is, Mom—doesn't mean I'm going to be dragged along with you. If you think Edgar Evernever is the key to being 'emotionally healthy,' you're fooling yourself. But you're not fooling me." I turned to face her, breathing hard. The drugs made everything hard and bright, like crystal. They kept me sharp. Even when my mother was loonier than ever.

"I know you haven't been Archie's biggest fan. But I don't care. He's my best friend, Mom, and that isn't going to change just because of what's going on—"

"He's <u>on trial</u>, Betty."

"You and I both know that Archie is innocent. And we're going to prove it. So don't try to stand in my way."

Her eyes welled up, and for a minute I could see my mother's heart, the part of her that loves me, that will always think of me as her baby, her perfect girl who needs protecting. She looked sad and vulnerable. It almost made me reconsider how I was—however inadvertently—hurting her.

<u>Almost.</u>

"Don't you get it, Betty?" she asked, pleading. "It's not about whether or not I like Archie Andrews—though, I'll admit, I haven't been crazy about his behavior in the past. Also, the boy's <u>crazy</u> for having never asked you out."

"Mom!"

She put up a hand to shush me and went on. "It's not about that, it's never been about that. Not really. But Archie's in trouble. And that means you could be, too." She moved toward me and I froze. She reached out for my hand, and with her other hand brushed an imaginary stray hair from my forehead. "I'm your mother, Betty. Protecting you will always be the most important job I have. And I will do anything to keep you safe."

Despite myself, I swallowed hard and let her pull me into a hug. She smelled like rosewater and fabric softener. "Mom," I said, moving away again after a beat, "that's the thing. You can't protect me. Bad things have happened in this town—to us! The Black Hood came to Riverdale. And it turned out he was one of us. He lived under our roof, with us. He was your husband. He's my father. My blood. One of the worst things this town has ever seen—and this town has seen some horrible, horrible things—and it was a part of us. And there's just no way to protect me from that truth."

That was it. Plain fact. Those were the feelings I couldn't process, the ugly whispers that wove through my brain at night.

"I love you, Mom," I said, "but I am defending Archie. Whether you like it or not. I'm going to do everything I can to keep him safe." I smiled. "Sound familiar?"

She laughed reluctantly. "You may be your father's daughter, but you sure are my daughter, too." She squeezed my hand. "And don't forget it. God knows this year has been grueling, but you are not your father. You can't think that way."

I didn't have an answer for that, so instead I deflected. "I'm going out," I said.

She sighed. "Just promise you'll be careful, Betty."

"Be careful." What did that even mean? I was working to prove Archie innocent, knee-deep in a murder trial. I'd caught the Black

Hood myself. I was so far past careful, it wasn't even in the rearview mirror. But I couldn't say that. So instead I just gave a small nod.

"Horrible things <u>have</u> happened in this town, Betty," she said, her voice tight. "More than you'll ever know."

I shivered. I didn't know what she was talking about. But for once, I wasn't even sure I <u>wanted</u> to know. The whole truth was turning out to be unbearable. Unimaginable.

My phone chimed. I glanced at the screen. "Jughead's outside," I said. "I've got to go."

CHAPTER FOUR

JUGHEAD

I'm weird. I'm a weirdo. It's practically my mantra; it was the first thing I said to Betty after we got together. It's important to be up-front about these things, especially when you're the "beanie-wearing cad defiling the girl next door." (To quote her mother, who certainly has a way with words. Then again, she's a writer, too. Bizarre to think Alice Cooper and I have anything in common beyond Betty.)

But anyway. Betty knew what she was getting into, dating Riverdale High's own personal J. D. Salinger. And though I like to play things low-key, I was beyond relieved—happy, even, despite not exactly being the shiny, happy type—that she not only wanted *me*, but she agreed to be my Serpent Queen when my father retired from the gang. Was I planning to take over the Serpent reins? No, of course not. Not at first. And there were . . . complications, drawbacks to the role. We Serpents have a reputation, even if it isn't always completely earned.

But a snake never sheds his skin. I'd learned that. And the Serpents? Well, they'd had my back when I had nothing, when everything else felt like it was falling apart. They say blood is thicker than water, sure. But sometimes found family is thickest of all.

So, Betty was being loyal to me, and we both were loyal to the Serpents. Which felt more crucial than ever now, with Hiram Lodge's plans to take down the Southside still murky and undefined (but no less suspicious), and with the gang displaced, relegated to a makeshift shantytown on the edges of the Northside.

And *that* didn't send Betty running? The girl was truly the Hepburn to my Tracy.

I owed her some loyalty of my own. Which is how a certified loner straight from central casting—a beanie-wearing cad such as myself—happened to end up at a raging kegger at the house of Reggie Mantle, the personification of "the Jock" from every generic eighties high school dramedy.

Just as long as I could get through the night without adopting a wise old mentor, learning the ancient warrior art of karate, and gliding through a sweeping training montage set to a new-wave medley, I'd be okay. *Fine*, anyway. Betty was worth it. Katharine Hepburn had nothing on my girlfriend.

Except, I'd lost her.

Not in any tragic, permanent sense. Just that we'd gotten separated. But that was bad enough. Maybe there wouldn't be a martial-arts-training-montage thing, but there *would* be that thing of the misunderstood indie boy dodging the cool kids in pursuit of a girl.

It wasn't the story line I'd been hoping for when I agreed to come out tonight.

I picked her up from her house, just like we'd planned, texting her from outside to let her know I was there. Not because I have no sense of chivalry, but because that had been Betty's explicit instruction, knowing as she did that her mom would give some pushback about the plan to go out, have fun, and try to be a normal teen within the Wes Craven house of mirrors freak show our once-idyllic town had become.

We rode my bike over to Reggie's, and when I pulled up, she got swept into something with Kevin Keller. It was awkward, I think, given his dad was the former sheriff, and Betty was working so hard on Archie's case. The sins of the father being visited on the son, and all that. Betty was above that stuff, but that didn't make it less weird sometimes with some of our friends and classmates.

I killed the engine and watched from a distance while she said her hellos, noticing the way her shoulders did that little hunch thing that happens when she's feeling stressed but trying not to show it. And meanwhile, the whole point of coming in the first place was to have fun and relax.

Too bad my own skin was already crawling.

Archie and Veronica weren't here yet, and that was basically the beginning and the end of my so-called social circle.

Reggie's garage door was propped open. It was a total mob scene in there. Even though it felt like walking directly into the belly of the beast—insane under the best of circumstances, which this clearly was not—I headed into the house.

Inside, I tried to think if I'd ever been to Reggie's before. We weren't exactly buds. We had the Archie connection, which meant that Reggie *usually* avoided harassing me as badly as he was probably inclined to do. Usually. (What a prince, right?)

But still, he was such a sleaze. I mean, it wasn't too hard to see why—his parents were certifiable; he never really had a chance. But, you know, we all have our parental crosses to bear. Why should Reggie get a pass on human behavior?

You're here for Betty, I reminded myself, taking deep breaths. The air smelled thick, like sweat and beer. *It doesn't matter whose house it is.*

And it *didn't* matter. It would have been deeply unpleasant, regardless.

But where *was* she?

I threaded through the bodies, everyone sticky and slick in the tight, humid space. I didn't recognize anyone . . . No, wait, there were those two River Vixens, the ones anointed as Cheryl Blossom's minions when she wasn't off making like Jack Kerouac with Toni Topaz.

I rounded a corner, seeing a door that looked like maybe a bathroom, or a closet . . .

. . . and bumped right into Ethel Muggs.

"Jughead! Sorry!" she stammered. Her cheeks were red and her eyes darted past me, over my shoulder, nervous.

"Hey, Ethel. Don't worry, you're good. I'm the one who wasn't watching where I was going. Sorry. Looking for Betty. Have you seen her?"

"No, sorry," she said. "I was looking for Ben. Or Dilton?"

"Dilton Doiley?" I tried not to sound as surprised as I felt. Hard to think she'd find him here. Suffice it to say, Riverdale High's very own Survivorman was maybe the only person less likely to be at a high school rager than yours truly.

"Um, yeah." There was an edge to her voice, like she was defensive. That I was surprised she'd be looking for Dilton? Or maybe I was being paranoid, imagining things. It was so stuffy in the house, my brain was fuzzy. I needed to find Betty.

"Dilton, Ben, and I were supposed to meet here," Ethel explained, so maybe she *was* feeling defensive. I filed that information away for later, when I'd have more bandwidth to think, just in case. If there was one thing Betty and I were great at, it was getting to the bottom of weird situations. We'd had so much practice lately . . .

"They're late. They said they'd be here half an hour ago, and I'm ready to leave. I'm pretty sure someone just threw up in a potted ficus back there." She grimaced.

"Yikes. Okay, yeah. You should find them and split. There's something like a thousand people crammed into the garage," I said. "Maybe check and see if either of them are stuck out there?"

Her forehead relaxed, like I'd reassured her somehow. "I will. Thanks. Good idea, Jughead." I remembered how she'd been a huge part of the group that brought down the pigs on the football team during that whole "scoring" thing, when Chuck got into it with Betty. It still made me go full Hulk—Lou Ferrigno Hulk, original flavor—thinking about that. And Ethel had been strong, brave. There was more to her than met the eye.

If she did find Ben and Dilton, I hoped they were ready for her.

"Good luck," I told her, glancing back to that door I'd seen. No one had come in or out while Ethel and I were talking. I still had no idea where Betty was.

"Check upstairs," Ethel said, reading my mind and pointing past the door. "If she's not in there, I mean. There's another bathroom upstairs. And all the bedrooms, you know. Maybe it was just too loud and crowded down here and she needed some quiet."

"Too loud? Here? You're talking crazy, Muggs." I shouted it to make my point. That coaxed an actual smile from Ethel, and we separated, each in search of our own distraction.

I knocked on the door and then leaned in, cupping an ear. I didn't hear anything, but that probably had more to do with the deafening roar swirling around me. I knocked again, louder, and leaned closer, even though I knew it was pointless. I grabbed the doorknob and twisted it, seeing if it was locked. The door sprung open.

"Excuse you, sir. Do you have something against knocking?" It was Josie McCoy, discreetly fluffing the edges of her spring-loaded curls. Her signature pussycat ears sat slightly crooked on her head, and she adjusted them, then wiped at something invisible beneath her eye.

"Sorry, I didn't realize it was occupied. But also: Locks are good."

"Thanks for the tip," Josie said with an eye roll. "I tried, it must be broken. Anyway, you might want to find another place to powder your nose." She was being clipped, standoffish, even by her usual pop diva standards.

"I'm just looking for Betty—" I started. But I stopped abruptly when I saw who was in the bathroom—who'd *been* in there, I mean—with Josie. "Sweet Pea?"

I mean, the only thing that might have surprised me more would have been if Josie had come out of the bathroom with one of the replicants from *Blade Runner*. Or, I don't know, Jigsaw from *Saw*. Actually, in Riverdale, that was probably slightly more plausible.

It must have shown on my face, because Josie looked pissed. Sweet Pea sidled past her. "Jug. Dude, just . . . be cool." He gave me a loaded look that was hard to take too seriously, given the smudge of stray lip gloss on his chin.

I held my hands up. "Totally. Ice-cold. You know me. A vault." I mimed locking my lips shut with a key. And I would be—completely mum. I knew all about unlikely couples, and I personally didn't need to out this one before they were ready. "Mea culpa."

"We were just leaving, anyway," Josie said. "I'm meeting my girls."

"I thought . . ." I trailed off. Was it my business whether the Pussycats were on-again or off-again?

She caught me catching myself and gave a wry grin. "Special engagement tomorrow. One night only. So for tonight, we've got some pre-gig hijinks planned."

"That sounds exhausting," I said. "Better you than me."

I felt that way about most stuff. It was a motto that had served me well in life, so far.

CHAPTER FIVE

ETHEL

Maybe this is a test. The Gargoyle King does like to challenge us. He wants us to prove our loyalty to him, our worth. And I am up for the challenge. Eager for it, even.

In some ways, it feels like everything—all the painful, disparate events of my life—they've all been leading to this, to the Game. Finding my own name in that notebook Chuck and the football team were keeping. Finding out my father had lost our life savings—and that the person who'd cheated him out of it was the father of one of my newest friends. That we were all linked in this unrelenting, pitiless ugliness.

My father's attempt to take his own life. Watching him struggle to recover. Watching my mother grieve and fret. Lying in bed, staring at the ceiling, night after night, praying he'd be okay. That we would all be okay.

Struggling every day—all of us, in ways big and small—now that our nest egg is gone. Giving up extras and frivolous luxuries. Letting go of the so-called nonessentials that make day-to-day living that much more bearable. Tiny, special joys—all of which were stolen from us.

But the Gargoyle King? He doesn't take, he *gives*. He makes promises. He whispers to us, seductive. He tells us we can have those joys, those luxuries back—if only we prove our loyalty.

So I do it. When the tasks are revealed, I revel in them, in my chance to rise among the group, within the King's eyes.

In the Game, I've found the things I want, I crave. A community, a purpose. A sense of higher order governing us all. The only thing that still remains just out of reach?

Dilton Doiley. And Ben, my prince.

It took me by surprise, too.

A chill settles on my back, in my bones, now, as I make my way from Reggie's house. Another dark night in Riverdale, another shadowy side road in this traitorous town I call home. I don't believe any of us are truly safe here. When a twig snaps in the distance, I flinch. But realizing it was only the wind doesn't offer much solace.

Jason Blossom's killer is dead. The Black Hood is behind bars. In theory, the evil that lurks beneath Riverdale's streets has been contained.

But just in theory.

I know darkness. It trails me, seeks me out.

When the boys—first Dilton, and then Ben—when they found me and recruited me into their game, I had hoped . . .

I had allowed myself a slight flicker of optimism, that if

Dilton . . . well, if he saw something in me, if he only . . . *noticed* me like I had noticed him . . . well, maybe then, the hope was that together we might be a force stronger than the darkness.

I didn't expect to have feelings for Ben. I didn't expect any of it.

The Game connected us. In Fox Forest, down in Dilton's bunker . . . we were working for the King, the three of us. Ascending, though we didn't use that word, not then. But in the process, we were binding ourselves together, weaving ourselves into a fabric I used as a lifeline.

I came to Reggie's tonight to see them. But I can tolerate the fact that they didn't come. It wasn't a set plan, after all. And I'm sure they're busy, involved in the Game, caught up in making sure the codes and tasks and trials laid out by the Gargoyle King are being met. That we're ready for them.

I trust Dilton. I trust Ben. And I trust the King.

And even though I feel a pulsing, panicking sense that again—as always—someone (or some*thing*) lurks in the beyond, in the Riverdale wilds . . .

I know, eventually, I will rise to the next level. I will be made whole. And Dilton will see me as the queen we all need me to be.

∧∧∧

VERONICA

It was a far cry from the heyday of Bungalow 8, but I had to hand it to Reggie—his little impromptu fete was fire. A gaggle of River Vixens were demonstrating our newest dance combo on the living room coffee table (I had to wince, hoping that the glass-topped Philippe Starck surface would hold up), the house was pounding with the steady thrum of bass, and beyond the living room, deep within the kitchen, I caught a glimpse of a handful of sweaty Bulldogs doing keg stands. I'd stumbled into my own personal John Hughes movie, and I was starring as the aloof privileged princess feeling supremely out of place among the hoi polloi.

I was here for Archie. The whole night had been for him, of course. But given his resistance, it was hard, with the swirling chaos and blur, to remember why.

I heard a questionable sound and turned to see someone hunched over a potted plant. Whoever it was obviously hadn't been pacing themselves. I saw another figure—a curl of auburn hair over the back of a collared blouse—*Ethel?*—tilt and react to it, too, then dart down the hallway. Before I could call out to her, someone flicked the living room lights down and raised the already-impossible volume on the sound system so the pulsating music felt like it was coming from inside my brain. To say I wasn't in the party mood was a profound understatement, and the feeling was intensifying by the nanosecond.

I swept through the kitchen as stealthily as I could manage and grabbed a cup of something bright red that I assumed was punch. I took a swig—liquid courage, a little instant happy, obviously I needed it—and shook out my hair, trying to release some of the viselike tension in my neck. I took another large drink, and the room blurred at the edges for a moment.

Air. I needed air. And three square feet of personal space, if that wasn't asking too much.

(It probably was. Was *everyone* at Riverdale High here tonight?)

I'd find a quiet corner, get my bearings, and track Archie down. I know we'd only just gotten to the party, but if he was having as much "fun" as I was—#verbalirony—maybe it was time to cut our losses.

∿∿∿

Upstairs, the Mantles' hall was adorned with family photos. It was like wandering through a time-lapse slideshow: Reggie's school pictures neatly lined in a row, a cluster of shots of the Bulldogs at their annual awards ceremonies. A tasteful wedding portrait, Mrs. Mantle looking barely older than Reggie today, swathed in delicate white lace.

One thing that was curiously missing in this gallery, I realized, was a picture of Reggie *with* his parents. The absence was fairly glaring, and it made it a little easier to sympathize with Reggie, to feel for him, despite his constant need to live out his own fantasy as the prototypical high school bully.

We all have our damage. And in truth, Reggie Mantle usually shows up when it counts.

Showing up. What I had tried to do, tonight—and every day since the arrest—for Archie. Was it all in vain?

Like an oasis in the desert, Archie's voice floated my way. I guess I wasn't the only one at the party looking for a little refuge.

Judging from his tone, it didn't sound as though he'd found it.

"I'm telling you, Betty. He was being totally aggro." The conversation was coming from a bedroom to my right. Reggie's room? Maybe. I'd never been up here before.

"He's *Reggie.*" I could hear the edge in Betty's voice, the slight strain that meant my bestie was doing her very best to be patient, even though she was on her last nerve. We all were. "Aggro's, like, his thing. It's just his way. You know that. It's all . . . bluster."

"Yeah, well, it felt pretty real when he was *blustering* in my face."

"You're overreacting."

"Am I? The last thing I need right now is to be thinking about him trying to cozy up to Veronica while I'm locked away."

Crap. Was *that* what Reggie had been bugging him about? I felt a little catch in my throat.

I'd heard enough. I burst into the room. I couldn't even bother pretending I hadn't just been eavesdropping.

"Excuse me, Sir Galahad," I said, waving a well-manicured hand at Archie. "Might I remind you that this damsel needs no knight in shining armor to rescue her from a dastardly foe. *If* Reggie Mantle ever decided to swoop in on yours truly, I hope you know I can more than hold my own." The drink I'd had burned a tiny ball of fire in my stomach, spurring me.

Betty held up a hand. "Relax, Veronica. Reggie was just trying to get under Archie's skin—*like he's known to do*—and Archie freaked a little. *Understandably,*" she went on, shooting him a look before he could protest.

Archie shrugged, those impossibly broad shoulders of his sagging in a way that made me want to scoop him up, brush his hair from his forehead, and make all sorts of promises I couldn't possibly keep about how everything was going to be just fine. "Maybe I freaked," he said. "I've . . . got a lot on my mind."

"That's an understatement," I agreed, moving to him. I wrapped an arm around him and snuggled against his chest. He felt warm and solid, and the thought of him going away so I wouldn't be able to see him, to fold into his arms, felt like too much to bear. "We all do."

I looked at Betty, whose eyes were red and troubled beneath those long, dark lashes of hers. "Betty, you've been working night and day on Archie's trial, and meanwhile, you've got your own issues at home."

She swallowed. "I don't want to make this all about me. But, yeah. My mom and Polly . . . they're impossible. They're not going to leave me alone until I agree to give the Farm—and Edgar Evernever—a chance." She shuddered. "They've been totally brainwashed, and they want to take me down with them."

"We *won't* let that happen," I replied, earnest.

"And what about you, Ronnie?" Archie pointed out. "Everything with my trial's been, like, the final nail in the coffin between you and your dad."

"No pun intended." The voice startled me, until I realized it was Jughead, in the doorway, a sardonic grin twisting the corners of his mouth. He nodded at Betty. "I found you."

"You were looking for me?"

"You vanished into thin air. I was forced to talk to people."

She smiled. "Sorry. I know you hate that. I just . . . it's so crowded downstairs."

He arched an eyebrow. "Tell me about it. I had the weirdest conversation with Ethel, and then—" He stopped abruptly. "Never mind. Let's just say, I've used up my social graces quota for the day."

"Honestly? Me too," Archie said. He looked at me, baleful. "I know how much you wanted us to get a break from everything, have a night out, Ronnie. But it's just . . ."

"It's not happening. I get it, Archiekins. Even a social creature as sophisticated as myself can sometimes make a bad call. And speaking of, how about we call it?"

"I feel bad, running out. You wanted so much for us to have fun, V," Betty said, biting her lip.

"Yeah, girl, exactly—I wanted us to have *fun*. Chugging spiked punch while randos hurl in the corner of the living room and our misguided host throws his extra testosterone around? *Not* fun. Ergo, we leave." A thought occurred to me. "But, that doesn't mean we have to go *home*. Who's hungry?"

As if on cue, Archie, Betty, and I turned to look at Jughead. He laughed. "Busted," he admitted. "I'm always hungry."

"Pop's it is," I said. "Driver is on call. He can come get us." I pulled my phone from my black Balenciaga, then frowned, realizing. "Except, I have no battery left."

I reached for Betty's phone in her pink quilted handbag— we're practically sisters, it was nothing I hadn't done a hundred times before—but she shrunk back, like she wanted to keep some distance between us. I tried not to give her a look, but I couldn't rein it in completely.

"Sorry," she said, catching the expression on my face. "It's, uh . . . buried in there. Let me get it for you."

"Sure." I tried not to stare while she fished the phone out of her bag, but it was impossible to avert my eyes completely. She must have been right—it definitely *was* way at the bottom, tucked underneath basically her entire life—because it took a few seconds of her pawing through the bag before she pulled it out.

I was trying to be discreet, but it was impossible not to notice.

I saw her hands, the scarred half-moon imprints where she clenches her fists when her feelings are too much to handle. Those hands closed around her bright pink plastic of her phone case, knocking aside—

Something familiar. Something totally harmless, completely benign, under the right circumstances.

It was a flash of orange plastic. The blur of a round white cap. A label, wrapped around a tube.

It was a *bottle*. A medicine bottle. In Betty's bag. Which, on its own, wouldn't have meant a thing.

But she hadn't wanted me to see it. She didn't want me to know it was there. That changed everything.

It wasn't the time or place to ask questions. But I knew what I'd seen, without a doubt. Mom's got enough pharmaceuticals in her medicine cabinet to enact an impromptu one-woman revival of *Valley of the Dolls*. I know what a prescription bottle looks like. I can open a childproof cap with my teeth. (Is it a cliché to say that it's one of the first things they teach you in private school on the Upper East Side? Because it is.)

Betty's mom had tried to put her on Adderall, I knew. Last fall, when school began. But Betty didn't bother to take it, always said she didn't like the way it made her feel like her heart was beating in her throat.

But that was then, this was now. And so many things had changed, for all of us.

Maybe Betty was changing, too.

She touched my elbow, interrupting my reverie. "Here," she said, handing me her phone. "Call your car. Let's get out of here."

CHAPTER SIX

Ethel:

> Where were you guys? I thought you were going to be at Reggie's tonight?

Dilton:

> Sorry, something came up.

Ethel:

> The streets feel dangerous tonight. Something heavy in the air.

Ethel:

> I think I'm being followed.

Ethel:

> I'd feel better going someplace safe.

Dilton:

> I can't meet you right now. Head to the bunker, it's safe there. Ben will be by as soon as he can.

Dilton:

> And stay alert.

HL:

Did the boy agree?

PP:

He's giving me pushback. I need more time.

HL:

I thought you said you had this under control?

PP:

My boys are loyal. He just needs a little convincing.
I think he's distracted. But he won't be for long.

HL:

For all of our sakes, I hope not.

Sweet Pea:

T! Why'd you have to pick the hottest weeks of
summer to hit the road? Trouble coming from all
sides. And all I want is to stay out of it.

Toni:

I'll bet you do.

Sweet Pea:

What's that supposed to mean?

Toni:

Are you forgetting I'm with Cheryl? Who's bffs with Josie McCoy? Consider, my friend, that I have eyes and ears. Which means none of your secrets are safe.

Sweet Pea:

Man. There are NO secrets in Riverdale. But I don't care about that. It's the other stuff. Trouble. Serpent/Ghoulie stuff.

Toni:

Come on. I can't be getting into this from on the road. All I can say is—lay low.

Sweet Pea:

I'm trying. I don't know how long . . . certain people will be held off.

∿∿∿

ARCHIE

I felt bad, being so grateful when Ronnie suggested we leave Reggie's to go to Pop's. All she'd wanted was a break for us.

But Reggie's house felt like the wrong kind of break. Just a reminder of everything we stood to lose. I wanted to spend my last few days with my friends. But I realized I wanted to spend my last few days with *only* my friends. Not a bunch of Bulldogs cutting loose.

The ride to the Chock'Lit Shoppe was short. Short enough that Veronica and I didn't have to make too much awkward small talk. Our comfortable silences were a little less comfortable these days, with the arrest hanging over our heads. But tonight, right now, the quiet felt right.

Veronica leaned toward me. She rested her head on my shoulder and slid her hand into mine. "I think we made a valiant effort with that party," she said. "But I don't really need a huge crowd. This is better." She sighed.

I kissed the top of her head. "I totally agree."

The car swerved suddenly, jolting us. There was a squeal as the driver hit the brakes. Veronica bounced back into me.

"What's going on?" she asked, sitting up and brushing her hair from her eyes. The driver had pulled to the side of the road, engine idling.

"I apologize, Miss Lodge. A young woman just tried to cross the road without checking—she jumped into our path. I think she's a classmate of yours."

Veronica lowered the tinted window to see who he was talking about. It was Ethel Muggs, looking shaken and slightly out of it. In the moonlight, I could see dark hollows underneath her eyes, like she hadn't been sleeping well.

"Ethel?" Veronica called, unclipping her belt and leaning out the window. "Are you okay? What are you doing wandering in the middle of the road in the pitch-black? Auditioning for a scene in *Scream Five Thousand*? Not a great idea, girlfriend."

Ethel shook her head, seeming to come out of her trance. "What?" She looked at us like she was just now seeing us for the first time. "Oh, Veronica. Hi. I, uh . . . I got a little distracted."

"I'll say. Be careful." She beckoned. "Do you need a ride somewhere? Where are you going? Let us take you."

"No, I'm fine," Ethel insisted. There was a nervous look in her eyes. "I was supposed to meet Dilton. And Ben."

"Where?" Veronica asked, gesturing to the deserted road. "Come with us to Pop's; we're going to get a bite."

"Thanks," Ethel said. "Maybe later. I'm fine, really. You guys should go. It's not . . ." She glanced at the sky, shadows falling across her face. "It's not safe out here, I don't think." She lowered her voice to a hoarse whisper. *"He's watching."*

Veronica frowned. "Okay, extra points for the extreme creep factor, Ethel. I'll give you that. But who? Who's watching?"

Ethel shivered. "Never mind. I shouldn't have said that. It's fine. Just . . . go. Get inside. I will, too. I'll see you . . ." she paused. "Well, I'll see you at school next week."

Right. School next week, after Labor Day. Everyone would be there. And in theory, I'd be there, too. I'd see them all.

Unless I was found guilty.

Ronnie looked uneasy. "Okay," she said finally. "You're a big girl. But listen—text me if you need anything, okay? We'll come get you."

Ethel forced a smile that didn't quite reach her eyes. "Of course, Veronica," she said, her voice still soft. "You're a good friend."

She gave a small wave and continued down the road. We watched her get smaller as she wandered farther and farther off, looking confused and, to be totally honest, a little spooked.

"Shall we, Miss Lodge?" the driver asked.

"Uh, yes," Veronica said, closing the window. She turned to me. "I hope she's okay."

"She will be," I said. I sounded way more confident than I felt. I had literally no reason to believe that except for blind faith. "We all will."

I hoped that was true.

CHAPTER SEVEN

BETTY

Dear Diary:

I think Veronica knows.

I'm not totally sure, and I'm sure as <u>hell</u> not going to ask, but there was this…<u>moment</u>, this look she gave me when she went to use my phone. And I don't blame her, the way I freaked when she reached for my bag. It was nuts, of course she noticed that, but I couldn't help it. The pills, they make me shaky. But…I need them. Ever since they put Dad in jail, I'm not sleeping. And that's not an exaggeration. I can't remember the last time I've slept more than a half hour at a time. I spend hours in bed, just watching the minutes tick by on my phone screen, that blue light glowing in the dark, listening to nothing but the dark thoughts swirling in my head.

In the morning, when the sun finally rises, I watch the sky flare red, then gold, with a sinking pit in my stomach. My eyes are heavy and I'm tired in my <u>bones</u>, like just the thought of getting out of bed is physically painful. But I can't afford to give in, or give up. Not even on these summer days, with no school, and no job.

Other kids have summer vacation. But not me, not right now. I have to be working, all the time, to do what I can to help Archie. I can't let my guard down, even for a minute. It's Archie's <u>life</u>, his future, that's at stake.

So: the pills. And that horrible feeling like my veins are charged with electricity and my stomach is in free fall. Because otherwise, I don't know how to do this. And I <u>have</u> to do it.

The funny thing is, my mom's been trying to get me on Adderall for so long. Last fall, she was filling prescriptions for me that I never bothered to pick up. And yet, somehow I don't think she'd exactly approve if she knew I'd been forging my own prescriptions from a made-up therapist for months now.

Ever since Dad was arrested.

I don't know how I've been getting away with it, but I have. And I've managed to keep it a secret. Until now.

Veronica. She <u>saw</u>. She may not know <u>exactly</u> what she saw, but she knows what a prescription bottle looks like. And she knows <u>me</u>, so if I feel so completely not myself on the inside, she must see it, on the outside. Which means it's only a matter of time before I'll have to come clean.

"Earth to Betty." I'd spent the whole ride from Reggie's to Pop's in my own world. Now Jughead stepped off his bike and smiled. He gently took my helmet off, taking a minute to brush my cheek with his finger. "You in there? You were having a little <u>Westworld</u>-esque fugue state for a minute there."

"Sorry." I kissed him. "Spacey, not fugue-y. Distracted. Archie was so upset back there at Reggie's. Like he really thought there was a chance he'd lose V while—well, I mean, if—he goes away." I couldn't bring myself to say the word "prison." Saying it was too close to accepting it. We weren't there yet—we couldn't be.

Jughead shrugged. "You know her better. She's clearly devoted to him, but who knows? He could be—well, he could be gone for a while. Stuff happens."

"Don't say that! Stuff doesn't just 'happen,' Juggie. And Veronica loves Archie—she's not going to betray him. He'd know that if he didn't have other stuff on his mind."

"I just meant that I get why he'd overreact, that's all. I think he's allowed to be a little high-strung right now, all things considered," Jughead said. He slung an arm around my shoulder and walked me toward the entrance to Pop's.

"Okay. But we can't be. Even if that's how we're feeling. We have to be strong." That was what the pills were for, after all. They gave my heartbeats heartbeats of their own.

"Call me Iron Man." He flexed his bicep so it jumped where it grazed my back.

"My hero. I will gladly be your Pepper Potts." Thank god I could count on Jughead to keep it together.

These days, I wasn't sure I trusted myself.

∧∧∧

Inside, Pop's was quiet. People were still at Reggie's party, I guessed. Veronica and Archie had gotten comfortable in our regular booth, right by the door, and Veronica was chatting with Pop. Technically, he was her employee, now that she owned the place. That would take some more getting used to, even if Veronica was gracious about it.

"Betty, Jughead!" Veronica brightened, seeing us come through the door. The overhead bell chimed as it swung shut behind us. "I don't know how we beat you here. We had the weirdest run-in with Ethel Muggs." She made a face like she was still confused. "But anyway. We just ordered shakes. Do you want?"

"I'd rather eat," Jughead said, sliding into the seat across from them. "How about a cheeseburger, medium. And onion rings." He looked thoughtful. "Maybe some extra pickles. Half-sour."

Pop laughed. "Anything else?"

"Fries," Jug said, not missing a beat. "Extra crispy."

"I should have guessed," Pop said. "And for you, Betty?"

I looked at the tall, frosted shake glasses in front of Archie and Veronica. She had her favorite, a double chocolate. Archie's was a bright pink. Strawberry. My stomach turned as he sipped from the straw. Another side effect of the uppers: a constant swarm of bees living in my belly. Was that just how it had to be now, until Archie was for-sure safe?

"I'm actually not that hungry, Pop." It was beyond the truth. "I'll just share some of Jug's fries."

"That's what you think," Jughead teased, and I poked him.

"Really, nothing?" Veronica asked. She raised an eyebrow at me. She and I are not "dressing on the side" girls, usually.

"Really. I ate just before the party. A huge dinner."

Actually, I'd pushed some chicken and vegetables around on my plate until Mom deemed it acceptable to excuse me. Honestly, I couldn't remember the last time I'd eaten a proper meal. The thought made me queasy. Those swarming bees had better things to do than digest food. "Maybe just some coffee," I said. "Decaf," I amended, seeing the looks I was getting. Insomnia, Betty, I reminded myself. It's a thing. Like I wasn't already amped enough.

"One decaf, coming up." Pop slipped his pencil behind his ear, tucked his order pad in his front pocket, and went back behind the counter to start on our orders. I could still feel everyone's eyes on me. My palms ached from clenching my fists the way I do when I'm stressed.

The way I do all the time, these days.

"So, Ethel?" I asked, leaning my elbows on the table. "What was she doing?"

Veronica waved her hand. "It was…Well, maybe it was nothing. I hope it was nothing. But she was walking by herself, down the road, on that bend where it's not lit at all. She seemed pretty out of it. We had to swerve to avoid her." Her eyebrows knit together at the memory.

"Oh my god! But she's okay?"

"Yes, she's fine. Shaken, barely stirred. We offered her a ride but she wouldn't take it." She shrugged. "Like I say, très odd, but it didn't seem like there was anything for us to do for her, really."

"She said she was looking for Dilton. Or meeting him?" Archie put in.

"Hopefully she found him," I said. "Or someone."

Pop slid a steaming plate of French fries in front of Jughead, who immediately doused them in ketchup and dug in. Through a mouthful, he remembered, "She was looking for him at Reggie's, too. It seemed weird. Dilton, at a blowout house party."

"Ah, Riverdale: where everything always has to be weird." Veronica sighed.

"He was in here, tonight." It was Pop, topping off my barely touched coffee.

Jughead looked up. "Dilton was?"

Pop nodded. "With that boy, the one who worked at the Twilight with you, Jug." He pointed, and we realized we weren't completely alone in the diner.

Jughead swallowed. "Ben. Right. Ethel said she was meeting both of them." Jughead waved, but Ben was perched on a stool at the farther end of the bar and seemed lost in thought. "I didn't even know they were all friends."

"I guess we don't usually think about Dilton's friends," I put in, "other than the Adventure Scouts." But of course he must have had his people. People, like, I guess, Ethel and Ben.

"They were talking about some game. Gargoyles and…kings?" Pop shrugged. "They were being real quiet about it."

What the hell? We all exchanged a glance. That was…new and different.

"Dungeons and Dragons?" Jughead asked. "Now that you mention it, I could see Dilton being into something like that."

Pop considered it. "Maybe. But I really thought I heard 'gargoyle.' You guys don't know it?"

"Not me," Jughead said. We all gave equally blank stares.

"It's always something new with you kids," Pop said, shrugging. "I don't even try to keep up."

Jughead smiled. "Me neither, Pop. Me neither."

∧∧∧

Polly:

Betty, where are you? Mom said you went out with Jughead to some party?

Polly:

Edgar and some other friends were coming over tonight for a new moon ceremony. Mom was really hoping you'd be there.

Polly:

I know the Farm isn't your thing, but you don't have to be totally closed off to it, all the time.

Betty:

I'm good. Sorry Mom's disappointed, but I'm sure she'll get over it. I'll be home later.

Polly:

Betty, I really think if you would just give it a chance . . .

Betty:

I'm good. Phone dying. See you back at home later.

∧∧∧

Polly:

Sorry, she's definitely not coming.

Alice:

You tried, sweetie.

Alice:

We'll just have to keep trying. Harder, next time.

Polly:

What does "trying harder" even mean?

Alice:

I guess we'll know when we get there.

Polly:

She told me her phone was dying. I'm pretty sure it was a lie. Or an excuse to blow me off.

Alice:

Well, I tried to track her phone but she shut it off. Whether it was deliberate or not, I can't keep tabs on her right now.

Polly:

Mom, you know that's not okay!

Alice:

One step at a time, Polly. It's NOT okay . . . But it will be. I promise.

∧∧∧

POP TATE

I never do understand those kids, much as I try. Just when you think you've got one thing figured out, something else comes up, some different fad or drama or mischief.

I guess that's the one constant in this town. The mischief.

Although, calling it that maybe makes it sound less dangerous. Robs it of some of its bite.

That Jones boy, he was my regular customer even before he got so interested in writing that book of his. And he would be the first to tell you, he isn't exactly a ray of sunshine. But it wasn't until Jason Blossom disappeared that Jughead decided to dive deep, trying to understand Riverdale's dark history.

As if it were something to be processed neatly, to be understood.

Now Jughead and his crew have embraced the mischief. The blackness. But have they gone too far?

Some places are just evil. Does that make me sound like a superstitious old kook? Maybe, but I stand by it. My own father claimed to have a little bit of the "shine"—said he could see beyond what was actually here with us in the physical realm. And he would be one of the first to tell you that Riverdale has a shadow of its own.

From the original murder among Blossom brothers, to the sticky underside of the maple syrup trade. From the Riverdale Reaper to the Sugarman, all the way down to the Black Hood. To the Geraldine Grundys of the world, and the "Sweetie" monster sightings in Sweetwater River each summer . . .

And the drownings. All of them sudden. All of them unexplained. Too many to make sense of.

From the Serpents Native members being driven from their land, to the Blossom house burning to the ground at Cheryl's hand. From the live burials at the Devil's Hand tree, to all the stories teens tell when—*if*—they manage to escape from the Sisters of Quiet Mercy.

Each of these messy, sad links forms the chains that drag Riverdale down into the evil deep.

Now Archie Andrews has been touched by the stain of Riverdale. The one boy who shone goodness through and through has been caught squarely in the cross fire of the heart of this place.

I see these kids, day in and day out. I hear the highs and lows of their friendships. The agonies and ecstasies of their love lives. I know them, maybe as well as their parents, sometimes. Sometimes even more so. I'd do just about anything for them. Lay my life down if it came to that. But I can't save Archie Andrews.

Not if Riverdale's darkness has claimed him for its own.

CHAPTER EIGHT

FP:

Jug, you out with Betty?

Jughead:

Just grabbing a bite at Pop's, why?

FP:

Have you heard anything from Penny Peabody?

Jughead:

Not in ages. Wasn't expecting to. Why?

FP:

Good. Let's keep it that way.

Jughead:

You definitely don't have to tell me that.
Something going on I should know about?

FP:

I'm hoping not. But you let me know if she
contacts you for ANY reason. And if she does—
whatever she asks, you say no.

Jughead:

Got it. And bonus points for use of cryptic rhetoric. Very evocative.

FP:

This isn't a joke, boy. Keep your head down and your nose clean.

Jughead:

Scout's honor.

FP:

You're no Scout, Son. SERPENT'S honor.

Jughead:

Noted.

ᴧᴧᴧ

JUGHEAD

I knew it wasn't totally kosher to pledge Scout's honor when I hadn't been an Adventure Scout since the days of Little Archie and Little League (and even then, I wasn't much of an active participant). But whatever noise Dad was hearing from the streets, he was legitimately worried about me getting swept up in something. Promising to stay out of trouble felt like the only option in the moment.

Even if it was a promise I couldn't necessarily keep.

Staying out of trouble was relative. And it was way easier said than done once the Serpents were involved. And now they were displaced, and I was their leader. I'd avoid Penny Peabody—gladly—but "out of trouble" was never a guarantee.

Whatever Dad had heard about, it would probably float my way before long. These things usually did, eventually.

But for now, I had Betty, Archie, and Veronica, and we were blissfully free of Reggie Mantle's party, and the steam from my French fries wafted up, lacing the air with a salty tang that made my stomach grumble.

I grabbed a bottle of ketchup again and doused what was left of my fries, then stuffed a handful into my mouth. It was mildly Cro-Magnon, I'll admit, and when I looked up, all three of my friends were staring at me in various states of bemusement.

"I'm hungry," I said, shrugging. I mean, they knew me. They'd seen worse.

"When are you *not* hungry?" Veronica teased, taking a generous but still delicate sip of her shake. "Anyway, we're mostly ogling because we're impressed."

"Yeah, if the whole brooding-novelist thing doesn't work out, I can be a competitive eater," I said. "It's good to have options."

"Speaking of . . ." Veronica said, casting a subdued look down at her food. "As much as I wanted tonight to be an escape, the party was clearly the wrong call."

It was a tenuous segue at best, and anyway, fairly unnecessary. I gestured to the burger Pop placed on the table in front of me, right on cue. "All's well that ends well?"

"Well, I appreciate that," she said. "But speaking of options." *There* was the segue she was building toward. "The party was the wrong one. And beyond that . . ." She shifted, uncomfortable in her seat. "Beyond that, it's looking like we may be *out* of options. For saving Archie." Her whole body tensed with worry.

We all sat, steeping in the heavy silence of that truth.

"I'm sorry, I *hate* to be the harbinger of doom, guys," Veronica said, her voice breaking. "But I just . . . I don't know. As much as Reggie was behaving like a Neanderthal, going on about stealing me away from you, Archiekins—"

"As if he could!" Betty put in.

Veronica nodded and continued. "Well, despite all his bluster, there *is* the bleak reality of Archie's potential incarceration bearing down on us. And I guess . . . I guess I thought one night out would relieve the pressure. But instead, it only put into sharp relief just how truly out of options we may be."

Archie took her hand. "I love that you tried, Ronnie." He looked at us. "You all did. Heck, Jughead braved a *house party*. That's friendship."

I offered a joking little bow. "Like a true warrior. A king." I took a beat. "A gargoyle king, if you will?"

From the corner of the diner, where Ben was sitting, I heard a clatter. When I looked over, he was scrabbling to wipe up his spilled milk shake. And if I didn't know better, I'd say his hands looked a little shaky . . .

Betty shuddered, and Veronica pulled her little cardigan more tightly over her shoulders. "I will not," Veronica said, clipped. "No, thank you."

"Jug, that's not funny," Betty chided. "I don't love the idea of Dilton Doiley getting heavy into a role-playing game that has dark undertones."

"You'd love it even less if you'd seen the look in Ethel's eyes tonight," Veronica said. "Dark undertones all around." She wrapped an arm around Archie and snuggled closer to him, like by doing so she could protect them both.

If only.

"No."

The table rattled, making me flinch. It was Betty, slapping her hand down with fury. It was like she'd just woken up, or been startled by an epiphany.

"No," she said again, louder now. "I don't accept that. Not about Dilton and Ethel, although it is a little weird and surprising," she said, reading the confusion on our faces. "But what you were just saying, Ronnie. About Archie. I refuse to accept that we're out of options."

"Betty, I mean, me too. But the only thing left is the closing arguments," Archie said, his voice strained. "And you know as well as anyone that my mom's as prepared as possible, but . . ."

". . . but she's up against the devil incarnate," Veronica filled in, "aka my father, Hiram Lodge. Who won't hesitate to play dirty if it means he gets his way."

Betty's eyes filled with tears. "I don't care. We have to do *something*. Something more, I mean."

"More than what you've been doing? You've been working around the clock. Betty, it's your summer vacation," Archie protested. "And you've spent it on my case." His voice softened. "Look, you've done all you can do. You've done more than anyone could possibly have asked of you. You're an amazing friend. An amazing person. But maybe Ronnie's right. Maybe now, we're out of options. Maybe now, we just wait."

I felt it then—that little frisson, that charge that runs down my spine when Betty and I are on the scent of something. Maybe it's not so romantic to think of myself and my girl like a pair of bloodhounds on a hunt. But it's one of my favorite things about us. We're like Watson and Holmes. Or—as Betty would probably say—like Nancy Drew and Ned Nickerson.

And we *don't* give up before we've cracked a case.

Under the table, I took Betty's hand. It was curled into a tight fist—I knew she'd have indentations from her fingernails later tonight. Gently, I opened her hand and held it against my knee. Her fingers radiated heat, like her pulse was pounding in my own bloodstream.

"Out of options is *not* an option," she said, steely and resolved. "There's always something else. Something more. And I'm not giving up on you, Archie."

"Hear, hear," Veronica said, raising her near-empty shake glass. "What did you have in mind, girlfriend?"

"Shadow Lake. It's where Cassidy was killed. Literally the scene of the crime."

"Lodge Lodge . . . or, in the woods nearby," Veronica said, nodding. It was the clever name her family had for their lake house. Once the location of idyllic family getaways. Now the site of Archie's potential downfall.

"So, who do we think killed Cassidy?" Veronica asked. "After Archie chased him out of the house?"

It had been a home invasion gone bad, four hooded thugs from town deciding to rip off the rich vacation-home owners who supported their town financially but infested the atmosphere like trendy cockroaches, pervasive and resistant to all efforts to keep them in their place. I don't know why Cassidy and his friends picked Lodge Lodge that night—maybe just seeing us in their shop in town, loading up on provisions, looking every bit the privileged snots on a weekend jaunt, straight out of central casting? When they broke in and terrorized us, there wasn't time to ask questions. And then Veronica pushed the silent alarm, and Archie ran the guys out of the house . . . and then there were gunshots. Two. We all heard them, though we didn't see a gun being fired.

"Archie, you saw Andre in the woods?" Veronica asked now, referring to her father's driver, the sometime security guard who replaced the Lodge family butler, Smithers, when Smithers was otherwise occupied . . . or when a job required a little more elbow grease than Smithers came by naturally.

"Yeah." Archie was curt, his forehead wrinkled. "I don't know . . . exactly what happened. I heard the shots, same as you guys, and then I saw Andre. And he told me it was taken care of."

"But what did he *mean* by that?" Betty asked. It was the question we'd all spent countless hours turning over and over together. "That he killed Cassidy?"

"Maybe. Probably. It wouldn't shock me if murder was considered a prerequisite for working for Daddy. It would explain why someone as kindhearted as Smithers needs backup."

"So Andre kills Cassidy . . ."

"And Daddy frames Archie. It's alarmingly straightforward in its duplicity, as far as evil plots go."

"But we can't prove it," Archie said, running a hand through his hair so it stood up in thick tufts.

"We *haven't* proven it *yet*," Betty corrected, giving my hand another squeeze under the table. "That doesn't mean we can't. Look, it's totally possible that somehow, we overlooked something."

"The police went over the crime scene with a fine-tooth comb," Archie said.

"Did they?" Betty countered. "We know that's what Mr. Lodge said. But we also know firsthand that cops can be bought off. Plus, if there's one thing we've learned, it's that Mr. Lodge is not . . ." She glanced at Veronica, hesitant.

"He's not the most reliable narrator," Veronica confirmed, her gaze hard. "To put it lightly." She tapped her fingernails on the table. "You guys, I think B is right. It's a long shot, yes, but it's a *shot*. And we have to take it."

"So, what now?" I asked, having a pretty good idea what the answer would be.

"Now we go back," Veronica said. "To where it all happened. We're going to tear those woods apart until we find something. Something that will prove, unequivocally, that Archie is innocent.

"We're going back to Shadow Lake."

∧∧∧

ETHEL

The sacred space is belowground, of course. As all such spaces are—removed, secreted away from hapless innocents. Those who would intrude. Those who would obstruct us.

Evelyn says that Betty Cooper is one such potential intruder. And though she and her friends have been loyal in the past, now, with the Game . . . my own loyalties must lie elsewhere.

Dilton built this chamber, a haven for our circle, those of us who wish to ascend to the Kingdom. The king's scripture doesn't demand it of us, his loyal subjects, but to embrace this clandestine hideaway affords us an extra element of the unique. It elevates us.

I check my phone. Nothing new from Dilton. He told me to stay underground, to stay safe. So, I will. I will prepare the space for him, for Ben. For the others we welcome—carefully, cautiously, with intention—into our circle.

I change, removing my pedestrian "street" clothes and shrugging on Princess Etheline's ethereal robe. It's light, gauzy, hand-stitched with effort and care. I light the candles, smoky-sweet, cedar and incense. The bunker glows in the flickering warmth of the light. I twist my hair into the slimmest crown of braids.

The first game is a player's point of entry. The portal to a realm of gryphons and gargoyles. To the magical kingdom of Eldervair.

Choose your avatar: Radiant Knight, Arcanc Invoker, Hellcaster.

We've chosen already, we three. The Princess, she is mine. Ben chose Hellcaster. We were meant to ascend together. But there've been whispers, lately. He and Dilton . . . do they have plans of their own?

There's a nagging claw of worry, a thorn in my gut. I try to push it away, to have faith. But still, I do wonder . . .

Will I be left behind?

No. They wouldn't. I have to trust. This game, this realm—it's ours, together.

I ready the quest cards, fanning them across the small folding table.

I fill the chalices. Fresh-Aid. Blue, of course. Will tonight be our time?

I settle in. I breathe. I wait.

PART TWO: THE LAKE HOUSE

CHAPTER NINE

Welcome to Shadow Lake!

Your membership to this exclusive community guarantees you the serene tranquility and peace of mind that comes with knowing you've invested in both quality and security.

Individual homes in our community are not numbered. Your mailing address will be provided in your new member packet, and should be shared only with trusted confidants to protect the uncompromising privacy of our group.

Our spacious, intelligent-design development plots offer discretion and seclusion, but rest assured the premises are under full-time surveillance via our private security team. Your safety is our priority!

As a Shadow Lake homeowner, you'll be asked to complete a nondisclosure agreement ensuring your commitment to our community bylaws. Compliance with our bylaws is mandatory, and any infraction will be subject to immediate review by our homeowner's board. Violators may be evicted, effective immediately. By signing this document, homeowners waive potential claims to future damages in the event of termination of contract.

The history of Shadow Lake is rich and storied. First established in the early 1920s, Shadow Lake itself soon became synecdoche for Northeastern urbanites seeking summer escape and mountain air, eventually competing with both the nearby Berkshire and Catskill regions for hard-won luxury tourist dollars. What set Shadow Lake apart was its boutique resort, The Overlook Lodge, located at the peak of Mount Phoenix. The Overlook sought to distinguish itself from oversized, all-inclusive hotels by maintaining a small footprint with just ten private rooms, each with en-suite baths, fireplaces, and on-demand gourmet room service. Eventually, it came to be recognized as a premiere alternative to mountain bungalow-colony vacationing.

Tragically, the original Lodge was destroyed in 1977, when an unwell caretaker engineered a total collapse of the building's boiler. The incident was officially deemed an accident, though speculation abounds, continuing to this day. Local teens entertain ghost stories of the caretaker's spirit, suggesting it lingers along the banks of the water. Keep an eye out for "Grady" at midnight, yourself!

We have Lodge Industries to thank for the Shadow Lake community's renaissance. The corporation bought the ruins of the inn and all surrounding property after the fire, focusing on renovating the remaining homes for private sale and restoring the Overlook to its original rustic grandeur. These days, President and Chairman Hiram Lodge maintains what was formerly the original inn as his family's private residence. If you see him or his beautiful wife and daughter out and about in town, do say hi! Above all, Hiram is a family man with a strong sense of community. We're thrilled to know he's at the helm of this very special place.

▲▲▲

VERONICA

"B, your phone's been blowing up since we got in the car. Your mom?"

Betty gave a small, guilty nod, tapped away a few more times at her phone, and then slid it back into her bag. She looked at me from across the backseat of the car. "She's crazy, you know. She and Polly are all over me lately. They cannot handle that I want exactly nothing to do with the Farm and Edgar Evernever."

I rolled my eyes. "Girl, I get it. You know I know crazy parents. I don't blame you, either. You just told her you were staying at my place tonight, right? I mean, no mention of the lake house or anything?"

Betty smiled. "*I'm* not crazy, V. I know better than that. She's still freaking out. And if she's this weird about me 'staying at your house,' imagine if she found out we went to the lake instead." She made a "no, thank you" face like she'd just tasted something bitter.

I patted Betty's knee. "Never fear, my friend. She's not going to find out. *No one* is going to find out. We covered our tracks like pros. *Right?*" I leaned forward so that Jughead and Archie could hear me from the front seat.

Jughead had gotten his hands on a car through one of his Serpent connections, so he was driving us to Shadow Lake. Archie was shotgun, supposedly navigating, despite the fact that Lodge Lodge was *my* family's home, not his.

(It's so cute when Archie goes for machismo. Was it sexist to have the boys in the front seat and the girls in the back? Maybe. But I preferred to be hanging with my bestie, anyway. I decided girl power meant the right to sit wherever I damn wanted to in the car, even if I was the one with the literal keys to the so-called castle.)

"Right," Jughead confirmed. "Honestly, my dad was a little distracted, anyway. He didn't seem bothered that I would be staying at, quote-unquote, Archie's house."

"And *my* dad would've said yes to anything that involved, quote-unquote, normal teen behavior," Archie said. "He's so stressed about me, and the trial. I actually feel kind of guilty about it."

"Well, *don't*," I insisted. "This is our chance to find evidence in your favor, Archiekins. And assuming we do find what we're looking for, your parents will be thrilled—if only just this once—that we lied to them. I promise." I took a beat. "The ends justify the means. Truer words."

"That's Machiavelli, you know," Jughead pointed out. "So maybe not the *best* example of a role model."

"Desperate times call for desperate measures," I said, undaunted. There was an adage for every occasion, it seemed. And sometimes you have to play dirty in order to win—I'd learned that all too well from Daddy.

"Well, these are definitely desperate times," Betty said. Her hands were clenched in her lap. I knew her body language almost as well as my own by now—she was dangerously close to going full dark.

And she wasn't the only one. There was tension in the car, a live wire so potent it could have powered the Las Vegas strip. I didn't want to think about what might happen if our "desperate measures" failed.

"So what *are* we looking for?" Jughead asked, casting a quick glance over his shoulder. The car swerved ever-so-slightly in the direction that his neck turned.

"Eyes on the road!" I pointed.

"Yes, Miss Daisy," he said. He focused, laser-sharp through the windshield. "God, it's pitch-black out here," he said. "Talk about full dark, no stars."

"Funny," I said, "I was just thinking about that." Even though it wasn't remotely funny at all. But maybe slightly reassuring that the four of us were so totally on the same page.

"Arch," Jughead went on, "this is the same road we took, that night. With the . . . uh, you know, the delivery for Penny Peabody."

"Yeah," Archie said, his tone clearly indicating how little he relished the memory. "The turn to Greendale is just off that way." He jerked a thumb to the right. "What was it Penny said? *Greendale's not a place you want to be after dark.*"

"Yep. And she wasn't wrong." Jughead's eyes darted around again, taking in the scenery. "This could basically be the opening scene of half a dozen horror movies. *Joy Ride. Wrong Turn. Texas Chainsaw Massacre.*"

I shivered. The sky seemed darker, inkier than it had been even a few minutes ago, ominous. And even though we weren't too far outside Riverdale yet, it was *quiet*—even quieter than our sleepy town. The kind of quiet that comes before a deafening cataclysm. Though I wasn't the true crime/horror buff Jughead was, even I knew the phrase *too quiet*. And it was, even with all the nervous chatter between us.

"Maybe some music?" I suggested. "Archie, as shotgun rider, you're the official road trip DJ."

Archie leaned forward and fiddled with the car's ancient AM/FM radio. "Uh, there's no Bluetooth hookup or anything," he said. "No MyTunes or Songify. I think we're stuck with whatever signal we can find." He twisted the dial and a sharp crackle of static split the air. Everyone jumped.

"Not less creepy than the utter silence, Arch . . ." Jughead mumbled.

"I'm trying . . ." Archie mumbled, hunched toward the dashboard. For a moment, the static settled. A deep, echoing voice boomed from the radio.

"And as the righteous shall be judged, so shall the wicked be punished. As it is written, so it shall come to pass."

"Oh, good," Jughead said. "*Children of the Corn*. Very comforting."

"About as comforting as your consistently gruesome references," I pointed out.

"I totally remember this station," Jughead went on. "It's the same one the creepy guy with the dead deer in his pickup was playing when our truck blew a flat, and I had to hitch a ride to complete my stint as part-time drug runner. Good times. Otherwise known as just your typical Tuesday night in Riverdale."

"Was it a Tuesday?" Archie asked.

"Don't be so literal, Archie," Jughead said. "My point was only that I'll start working on my sunny disposition when Riverdale stops being so . . . *Riverdale*."

"Okay, so when hell freezes over," Archie said.

"That's the thing, Archie," Jughead said. "Aren't you listening?" He gestured at the radio. "This *is* hell. We're already here."

"At least we're here together," Betty said, her eyes darting around the car. She seemed extra nervous, twitchy, even given the overall mood.

The orange bottle. Did Betty's nerves have anything to do with that? What wasn't she telling me?

We didn't keep secrets from each other.

Except for when we did.

There was probably a Machiavellian saying relevant to that, too, but I didn't want to dwell on it. Every now and then,

I have the nagging sense that maybe I'm more like my father than I care to admit. I pushed the thought down, deeper than the black hole we seemed to be driving straight toward.

"Anyway, we're not in Riverdale anymore, guys. This is Greendale," Betty said.

"Like maybe the one other town that could possibly rival Riverdale in weirdness," Jughead said. "I've heard stories. And not just from Penny Peabody."

"*There's* that bright side we were all so eagerly awaiting!" I chirped.

"Jug—*look out!*" Betty yelped as we swerved again, more dramatically this time, the car fishtailing and the brakes squealing. Betty flew against the side window with a thud I swear I felt, too. "Ow!" She reached up and patted the side of her face gingerly.

"Betty!" The car cut to the right once more, jerking straight past the glowing white line of the shoulder and into the dirt, kicking up clouds of dust that swirled like glitter in the car's headlights.

"Crap!" Jughead threw the car into park and stretched over his seat to get to Betty. "Are you okay?"

"I'm . . . fine. I'm okay, Juggie. Just a little stunned."

"Still, though." He hopped out of the front seat and opened the back door for a better look. He took her chin in his hand and gently tilted her head. "There's gonna be a hell of a bruise on this cheek." He kissed the area softly and Betty smiled, though she winced briefly at the contact.

"Everyone else okay?" Jughead asked.

We each stepped out of the car and took inventory. Archie had banged his knee against the dash; it was sore, but he'd seen worse injuries on the football field. I'd have a red mark in the shape of an old-school window crank on my forearm for a few days. Still, though. We were lucky.

"It could've been way worse, considering," I said. I rubbed Betty's arm. "As long as you're sure you're okay? I think you got the worst of it."

"I'm so sorry, guys," Jughead said, looking gutted. "I just—something ran out in front of the car."

"What, like an animal?" Whatever it was, it must have been small, since Jughead hadn't seen it at first. But it was hard to imagine a small animal could cause so much chaos.

"Yeah," Jughead said. "*That* animal, actually." He sounded surprised. "It came out of nowhere." He pointed.

It was a cat, average-sized and utterly pitch-black. "No wonder you didn't see it," I said. "It was perfectly camouflaged for a night like this."

The cat peered straight at us—like it could hear us, like it understood the words we were speaking—and blinked slowly. Normally I loved the green-gold color of cats' eyes, but in the dark, with nothing but the residual hum of the car engine and a chatter of crickets in the background, the cat's expression seemed unnervingly sentient.

"Well, if everyone's okay, and the car's running, too, we should probably get back on our way," I said. "The last thing we need is to be here if someone heard the car swerve and called the cops."

"But we didn't do anything," Archie protested.

I looked at him and raised an eyebrow, and he went quiet. I didn't have to say the words: We all knew firsthand that that wouldn't necessarily matter. It certainly wouldn't be the first time an innocent person fell victim to misplaced "justice."

"We did one thing," Jughead said. "I hate to point out the obvious, but we've literally walked into the opening scene of a Stephen King novel." He shooed the cat. "Scat." To us he said, "Nothing awesome follows a story beat like this."

The cat blinked again in that lazy, almost reptilian way, and my skin crawled. What was it I'd said about Riverdale, when I first arrived? That it was strictly *In Cold Blood*. "Okay, *auteur*. So what would the characters in this horror novel do if they were in our shoes?" I tapped the stiletto heels of my Louboutin peep-toe booties against the road for emphasis.

"Well, what they *should* do is get back in the car, turn around, and head right the hell back where they came from. Do not pass go, do not collect two hundred dollars."

"But that's not an option for us," Betty said, steely.

"Right. And it wouldn't be in the book, either. I'm just saying. It's what smart, reasonable people would do. So, not us." He smirked.

Meanwhile, Archie had wandered back around to his side of the car. "Uh, guys. Our options may be more limited than we thought."

"What do you mean?" Betty perked up, sounding concerned.

"The front tire's blown." Archie sighed. "We're not going anywhere until this is taken care of."

"Naturally." Jughead pulled his hat down tighter over his ears despite the thick, murky humidity of the night. "Wes Craven couldn't have written it better."

The cat gave a sinister hiss and finally leaped off into the shadows.

CHAPTER TEN

ARCHIE

Our options may be more limited than we thought. That's what I said when I realized we'd blown a tire.

It made sense, in a way, that this had happened—the cat, the swerve, the flat. It just seemed like everything had been going downhill for a while now. Like ever since . . . well, I didn't like to admit it, or to think too much about it—even, like, just in my own head—but ever since I made the mistake of cozying up to Hiram Lodge.

Everyone warned me against getting in too deep with him. Hell, even *Veronica* warned me away. That should have been the clincher. But he's her *father*, and . . . well, if I'm totally honest? I wanted my girlfriend's father to like me. It was that simple. That stupid.

And the worst part? Like, maybe even worse than what was happening to me, with the arrest and the trial (because, in some twisted way, at least that was happening to *me*, like consequences of *my* own behavior falling on *my* shoulders and *mine* alone)?

It was the fact that I'd betrayed my own father in the process.

I'd turned my back on my dad, the one person who's always had my back no matter what, the man I'd looked up to since I was old enough to form memories. And so, yeah, all the bad luck, the fallout, the blowback—everything that had rained down on me since I made an enemy of Hiram Lodge—it all made perfect sense. I deserved it.

But not my parents. Or my friends. No way.

But here we were, my friends and me. Stranded on the side of the road somewhere just outside Greendale—the Black Hood's original playground, among other things. And it was my fault.

"Jug, pop the trunk. Let's see if there's a spare back here."

"Archie, I love it when you go all grease monkey on us. It's so salt of the earth. The fanfic just writes itself." Jug hitched his jeans up and opened the front door of the car, feeling around for the trunk release until we heard the *click* and saw the car's hatchback peel open.

I unloaded the bags—there wasn't much, we were only going to be away for a night, and even if we wanted to stay longer, we didn't want anyone to see us with tons of stuff and get suspicious. My backpack, Jug's messenger bag, Betty's leather computer bag, a change of clothes peeking out where normally there'd be a laptop cord. Something heavy and expensive smelling and covered in monograms that Ronnie took any time she went away overnight. Once they were on the shoulder, out of the way of any cars that might pass by, Betty came up behind me and shone her phone's flashlight into the space.

"There, Arch," she said, showing the cutout in the floor of the hatchback. "Bingo. Spare storage."

I reached to pull the cover of the cutout up and Betty sidled closer, like we were surgeon and nurse in an operating room.

"Wait, hold the fanfic, I have a revision. I *adore* when my girlfriend goes all *Top Gear*," Jughead said. "Sorry, Archie, but you have to admit maybe you should let her take point on this."

I shook my head at Jughead's smirk, but he was right. I moved to make a little more space for Betty. "Do you want me to hold the flashlight? We shouldn't leave the car lights on; it'll drain the battery."

Betty smiled. "Thanks, Archie. This'll be a team effort. It's kind of an all-hands-on-deck situation, anyway."

"You're not kidding," Jughead said. There was something in his voice, a little pinch of dread, that made me turn. Behind us, a telltale white car with a blue light on the roof was bearing down.

"Who called the cops?" Jug asked.

"Maybe some Good Samaritan heard us, when we swerved and landed in the shoulder," Betty said. "Very helpful."

"Of course it would be the exact moment that we least need an actual helping hand," Veronica said. She glanced around, taking in the scene. "Jug, take off your jacket."

"What?" Jughead blinked. He held out his leather-clad sleeves—*A Serpent never sheds its skin*, that's what he always said when I gave him crap about wearing his Serpent jacket, like, *all the time*, even in the sweltering summer—looking surprised by what he saw.

"I'm thinking an officer of the law might be more kindly disposed toward us if we—"

"If you're not harboring a hoodlum in your midst," Jug said, getting it. "Sure."

"Desperate times," Betty said, quiet, like she was worried he was going to do the Serpent-shed thing, like usual. But she didn't have to worry about that.

It was maybe the *only* thing she didn't have to worry about.

The police car pulled up behind us and parked, leaving the lights flashing. An officer in uniform stepped out. He was older, like maybe our parents' age, with that beer belly that sags over a belt buckle after a certain point. He was big, like he'd played football once, maybe for the Bulldogs even, but not in a while. Not with that sag and those dark, shadowed circles under his eyes.

Whoever had called in our crash, he didn't look worried, or eager to help us. There was a weary glint in his eye, instead. Like he was wary of us. Suspicious.

"You kids all right?" His voice was low and gruff. Nothing about this guy was painting a picture of a man who'd want to give us the benefit of the doubt.

"We're fine, officer," Jughead said quickly. He kept his head bowed slightly and his voice low and a little hopeful, his "I'm being helpful" tone I remembered from grade school, when he was trying to fly under the radar of bullies like Reggie and his friends.

"Got a phone call that there was some noise, sounded like a car running off the road."

Which wasn't a crime, I wanted to point out. So there was no reason for him to be looking at us the way he was. But I didn't dare. Because underneath it all was the bare truth: I had been accused of *murder*. I was currently awaiting my *trial*. So however innocent I wanted to act right now? However much I wanted to protest, to point out that all we'd done was swerve to avoid hitting a random cat?

Well, any protest I might have made felt hollow. Because even if I hadn't killed Cassidy Bullock, I sure as hell wasn't *innocent*. If I were, we wouldn't be here in the first place.

"Well, yes, as you can see, we did." Betty stepped forward, smiling that little shy-girl smile, the one she gave grown-ups when necessary. Jug, Ronnie, and I knew her well enough to know that underneath that smile, she was so furious she was practically shaking. "There was a cat, it jumped out onto the road—"

"A *cat?*" the officer asked, like we were trying to pull a fast one on him or something. "Now, maybe if you'd said a *deer*, then maybe I'd have believed you. But running off the road, popping a tire . . . for a *cat?*" He scratched his chin slowly, carefully. "You can see where that wouldn't make too much sense."

"What I can *see*, officer, is that you seem way more concerned about harassing a group of innocent teenagers—who, I might add, are clearly struggling with car troubles—rather than offering us any assistance." Veronica's voice was clipped, sharp. She stared at the officer, daring him, asking him to please, *please* just push back.

"Ronnie," I mumbled, quiet. She was right, of course. He should've been checking to see that we were, actually, all right, rather than trying to poke holes in our story. But that feeling of guilt, of dread, it still sat in my gut, heavy and round like a bowling ball. I just wanted to play nice so that the officer would leave.

Unfortunately, Ronnie is *not* someone who just rolls over and plays nice for the sake of it. Especially not when the people she cares about are being targeted.

It's one of things I love about her. Even if her timing felt a little off right now.

"Miss, I think you're gonna watch your tone."

"Veronica—" Betty started, putting a hand out.

Veronica shook her off. "I think you'll find that *you're* going to want to consider how this low-level harassment will look to the mayor of Riverdale."

"Why don't you let me worry about the mayor, little girl? I doubt she'd trouble herself with something as trivial as this," he said, his tone more threatening now.

"Are you sure? Because I can call her." Veronica held up her phone. "She's right here, at the top of my contacts list. Under *Mom*. So if you wanted to give her a ring, see how she felt about your personal understanding of what may or may not be considered a *trivial* incident, I'm sure she'd pick right up." She beamed. "She always takes my calls."

"You're the Lodge girl, then?" The officer looked like he was making connections now.

"Veronica Lodge. The one and only." She held her hand out and he shook it, grudgingly.

"So, your mother is Hermione Lodge, the mayor," he went on, the last bits of the puzzle clicking into place.

Veronica nodded, still looking as cheerful as ever. That girl could be charming—when she wanted to be.

"And you're . . . Hiram Lodge's girl."

"Daddy? Yes. That's him. Do you know my father? Because if so, then you probably have some sense of exactly how well he'd take the news that his daughter had driven off the side of the road and the policeman who arrived on the scene was more interested in interrogating her and her friends than offering help."

I had big doubts about how much Mr. Lodge would actually care—especially these days, especially if he knew I was in the car, too—but the cop seemed to be buying Veronica's story. *That's my girl.*

"I asked if you were hurt," he protested, suddenly looking very worried. "That was the first thing I asked."

"True, true." She tapped a polished finger against her phone, teasing now. "So maybe it wasn't so much *what* you said, but the way you said it." She shrugged. "Or maybe I'm just imagining things. But you don't have to leave it to me!" She held the phone out, taunting. "Let's just give Daddykins a buzz. I'm sure he won't mind having his Saturday night interrupted with this news."

The cop sighed, and for a second there, *I* got worried. This guy could make real trouble for us. And I had more than enough trouble on my plate right now.

Or, if he *did* call Veronica's bluff and contact Hiram, then what? I didn't want to think.

"Veronica, I'm sure we don't need to call your dad." Betty stepped forward, playing at being the super-sweet girl next door again. "Someone called in what sounded like an accident. This kind officer"—she shot an extra smile his way—"came out to check up. He asked if we were okay, and we are." She turned to the cop. "We really appreciate your concern. But, as you can see"—she gestured—"we have a spare and we're all set."

"She's great with cars," Jughead put in, clapping Betty on the shoulder.

"We're actually on our way to the Lodges' home on Shadow Lake right now," Betty said, her voice loaded with meaning. "We'll be sure to let Mr. Lodge know how . . . *helpful* you were when we see him."

Damn, Betty could be good. Sweet girl next door . . . with a twist. Veronica nodded along approvingly.

The officer chewed on his lower lip. Finally, he opened his mouth like he was going to say something, and then closed it and sighed instead. "You sure you kids are okay, then? You don't need me to call for a tow, or anything like that?"

Betty shook her head quickly, looking grateful. "We're good," she assured him. "We've got this."

The cop left us, and it finally looked like we were ready to head to the lake.

∧∧∧

It wasn't until we were back in the car, Jughead behind the wheel but Ronnie shotgun now, to direct, that we realized. Well, *Betty* realized. All those years with her Nancy Drew handbook, I guess. She's way more observant than the rest of us.

We were driving along when she sat straight up and gasped. "You guys!"

Jughead jumped in his seat. "I love you, but please don't startle me, Betty," he said. "I like to keep my near-death vehicular experiences to one a night."

"He's kidding," Veronica said, even though, of course, Betty knew that. "I mean, about near-death, not about loving you, obvi. But what is it?"

"I just realized. The gray van."

"What gray van?" I had no idea what she was talking about, and it didn't seem like the others did, either.

"I think . . . I almost missed it myself. Because we were hung up, talking to the policeman, and he left his lights on. But I'm telling you, it happened: A gray van drove by while we were all talking. It seemed weird then. Because literally *no other* cars have passed, at all. And it was going slowly."

Veronica thought it over. "It's entirely possible I was so focused on getting Officer Krupke off our backs I didn't notice. Though, what you said: It's pretty deserted out here. We're not that oblivious. Are we?"

Jughead shrugged. "Not intentionally. But never say never."

"That's the thing," Betty said. "The police car lights were on and we were distracted. The van was gray, so it didn't stand out. And—I don't know, call me crazy, but I swear . . . when I say it was going slowly, I mean it, like, *coasted by*, lights off, when it drove past."

"Slowly . . . like it was casing the place?" I asked.

Betty looked grim. "Like it was casing *us*? I can't say for sure."

Veronica held up a hand. "B, you know I'm not calling your powers of perception into question—you've never steered us wrong before. But *no one* else saw it? It just feels . . . off. I don't know. I think we've all got horror movies on the brain."

"I mean, that literally was the opening scene to *Get Out*, getting run off the road and harassed by a cop," Jughead said. "These may be random coincidences, but they're not figments of our imagination."

Veronica shrugged. "Okay. I'm definitely not saying you *didn't* see that van. I guess the thing to do now is . . . just keep our eyes open. Metaphorically *and* literally."

Betty frowned. "They were open before," she insisted. "I think now we need to be on high alert."

"Done," Jughead said. "DEFCON one. Eyes open, extreme caution mode engaged. Operation: *Cabin in the Woods* is a go."

It wasn't a joke, but it was kind of the closest Jughead ever got.

And none of this was really funny, anyway.

Reggie:

Damn, girl, did you ghost on the party?

Josie:

Sorry, Mantle, but I told you it'd be a drive-by. My kitties and I have plans tonight.

Reggie:

A little hell-raising?

Josie:

What can I say? We're feisty that way.

Reggie:

Hellcats. Love it. Well, keep me posted on what you get into. Maybe we can meet up later.

Josie:

. . . Maybe. Don't you have a party to host?

Reggie:

For you, I'd rain-check. Send all these losers home.

Josie:

¯_(ツ)_/¯

Reggie:

Thanks?

Josie:

K, gotta run. TTYL. Have fun!

∿∿∿

Sweet Pea:

Didn't see you leaving Reggie's.

Josie:

Sorry, you were on your phone and I'm not trying to be obvious about this thing with us, you know. So it wasn't like I was gonna wait. Side note: You were texting like a crazy person. What's up with that?

Sweet Pea:

Forget it, not worth explaining.

Josie:

Sweet Pea:

Trust me.

Josie:

If you insist . . . I get enough drama on my own. TTYL!

∿∿∧

PP:

If you're not going to do this, you'd better find me another solution to my problem.

Sweet Pea:

. . .

PP:

Consider this your last warning.

CHAPTER ELEVEN

JOSIE

We may live in a small town, but that doesn't mean our ambitions are small. Take note: Josie and the Pussycats are destined for greatness—together or apart. You *will* see us all headlining in New York City sooner rather than later, I can promise you that.

(I know it's been rough riding since earlier this year, when the girls thought I was diva-ing out, pursuing my solo career. And yes, for a little while, one Veronica Lodge was seeking to inherit my throne . . . and my cat ears. But I still have hope that in the end, this litter sticks together.)

In the meantime, though, tomorrow night we were scheduled for a one-night-only, exclusive showdown against our Southside archrivals, Venom. A very different sound from the 'Cats, extreme postmillennial girl-grunge, but around here, we have a lot of crossover audience.

Playing against Venom in Centerville on a random summer night isn't New York City, not by half, but that didn't mean we weren't taking the gig seriously. We take *all* gigs seriously. That's why we rock them as hard as we do.

It may be a little-known feline fact about us, but we party hard, too. I know, I know—our voices are our instruments, and we "should," in theory, be cozying up with a cup of chamomile with honey the night before a performance. But that wouldn't be very rock star of us, would it?

Which means that's not who we are.

So we rock hard, and the night before a gig, we party. Hard.

Tonight was no different. After we did our little mandatory face time at Reggie's soiree (it's so important to connect with our fans in real time, after all), we headed straight to Venom's lair—the Southside.

"Hold on to your catnip, ladies," I told Val and Melody as we zipped down the highway in my red convertible— the unofficial Pussycat mobile.

It felt like old times. I tried not to let the nostalgia pull at me too hard.

"Kitty, you are beyond loco," Melody said. She reached out from where she was sitting, shotgun, next to me. For a second, I thought she was going to tell me to slow down, but instead she threw her hands in the air and whooped like a wild woman. She was feeling it, too. Cat scratch fever. Even if it was temporary.

"You know it, girls," I said. "Meow."

∧∧∧

BETTY

Dear Diary:

I'm not stupid.

I mean, maybe people tend to write me off sometimes as, like, the "perfect" girl. Maybe being the sweet, nice girl next door throws them off, makes them think I'm clueless. But even if I hadn't solved two different murders right here in Riverdale, I'd still tell you: <u>I promise you, I don't miss a thing.</u>

I'm not the dumb blond next door. I was right about the video in Jason Blossom's jacket lining. I was right about the real Black Hood. So when I say there was a sketchy van creeping down the road while we were getting questioned by that policeman? I know how it sounds. I know it seems random, and unlikely. And weird that I was the only one who caught it (and I didn't catch it—consciously, anyway—right away, either).

But that's our freaking <u>life</u>. Our town. Random. Unlikely. Weird.

I'm not stupid. I saw the looks Veronica, Archie—even Jughead, if I'm totally honest with myself—gave when I mentioned the van. They said they'd keep their eyes open, but deep down, they think I'm really just overreacting.

Maybe they're right. Maybe it'll turn out to be nothing.

But I don't think so. And I think, these days, I have to trust my gut.

So even if this road trip was all about recon, looking for evidence to prove Archie's innocence—even if we were all already on high alert? I'm taking it up to eleven. There's too much at stake for anything less.

∿∿∿

SHADOW LAKE GENERAL STORE, that's what the sign outside said. It was painted in bright red alongside the log walls of the Adirondack-style building. Everything in Shadow Lake had been built the same: Lodge-style, with dark wood and faux fur and fireplaces everywhere.

Normally, it would be cozy. The perfect mountain getaway, idyllic and charming in any season. That's what we thought the first time we came here.

Then those guys broke in, and Cassidy was killed, and everything changed forever.

I wasn't the only one who felt it when we first pulled up, that dark mass of memory creeping over us like a fog as Jug eased the car into park and turned it off. The crank of the parking brake was sharper than a crack of thunder in the small space. I realized how tight my chest was, how hard I'd been holding my breath, and sighed it out, and then the others did, too.

"Aren't there <u>any</u> other shops in town, Ronnie?" Archie asked.

"Believe me, Archiekins, if there were, I'd be all over it. The last thing I want to do is revisit the scene of the crime." Veronica paused, taking in the words she'd just used. "Or, to be more accurate, the scene of the <u>catalyst</u> of the crime. If Betty and I hadn't gone into town that that morning, if I hadn't been chatting with that random townie—"

"You were being friendly, V," I interjected. "There was no way to know he was a psychopath and a burglar." I meant it. Of course she had no idea. She couldn't blame herself.

It was so easy to tell other people not to beat themselves up. Too bad I couldn't take my own advice.

"Funny, you'd think we'd be a little better at recognizing those on sight, given all the practice we've had," Jug quipped. He saw my face. "Okay, it's not really funny," he admitted.

"None of this is funny," Veronica said, touching up her lipstick in the visor mirror. "But it's necessary. As is eating. A mission like ours requires sustenance. And this is the only place to pick up provisions without going twenty more miles north on a one-lane road. Or all the way back to Riverdale again."

"It'll be fine," I said, even though I felt my heart catch in my throat as I glanced at the front of the store. "Those guys aren't working here anymore. We'll be quick, just get what we need and get out."

I meant that, too.

I actually thought it would be that easy.

～～～

A bell over the door chimed loudly as we walked in. Another touch that would have been totally quaint under totally different circumstances. Instead it rang in my rib cage, rattling me like a bullet. This wasn't good. What happened to being sharp, to taking it to eleven?

I scanned the store: shelves of gourmet jam, cords of firewood, bug spray and flashlights and old-timey packages of popcorn that you popped over the fire so the tinfoil cover puffed up.

We were alone in here, but I heard it, still: whispers, a soft chatter, ominous and foreboding. The space felt haunted. I squeezed my hands into fists. I was having one of those fight-or-flight reactions, and every cell in my body was telling me to run.

"You okay, Betty?" Jug was asking. His voice sounded like it was coming from very far away. The store had tunneled, too, in my vision, so that all I saw was a small pinprick of light.

Get it together, Betty.

"I'm fine. I'm good," I said. "I think I just need the restroom. We've been in the car forever. I'll, uh, splash some water on my face."

"Bathroom's that way."

I let out a little involuntary shriek, which was embarrassing. But the speaker had appeared out of nowhere. Like a ghost.

She had pale strawberry blond hair pulled into a lank, greasy braid, and a flat, wide face. Her eyes were small and set deep above doughy cheeks. She looked highly unthrilled by our arrival. Even though we were the only customers in sight.

"Thank you." I tried to smile. She didn't smile back. Just gave me that steady, slightly sullen gaze as I made my way to the back of the store, to the door she had pointed at.

The bathroom was small, and the overhead fluorescent light buzzed and flickered. The faucet was rusty and dribbling a steady pulse into the cracked porcelain basin of the sink. I wanted to be out of here as quickly as I could, but my hands wouldn't stop trembling long enough to cooperate. I fished the prescription bottle out of my bag and fiddled with the childproof cap. My hands were so shaky, it took a few seconds, but finally it popped off.

I shook a few of the little blue pills into my hand. I sifted through, looking for one that'd been cut in half. A little boost was all I needed right now. I had to stay sharp—sharp<u>er</u>. And I was running out of ways to do that.

I swallowed the pill dry, feeling it catch for a second in the back of my throat. It didn't have a taste, not really, but my mouth was still rank and bitter. I turned the tap on and cupped some water, sipping it down. It was cold and metallic. I thought of dead leaves, wet piles left to rot in late autumn. The image made my stomach churn.

Turning the sink off, I caught sight of my face in the bathroom mirror. It was smeared with fingerprints and caked over with grime, but there were my eyes, bright and green, peering back at me. They looked suspicious. Thoughtful. Worried.

They looked angry, too.

They were my father's eyes, reflecting back at me.

I reached up, tightened my ponytail, and went back to my friends.

I didn't think I'd been in the bathroom that long, but when I came out, Veronica was already at the counter with her wallet out. The somber blond girl from before was there, behind the register, but she'd somehow multiplied: Standing next to her now was a boy who <u>had</u> to be her twin. It was almost funny how much they were carbon copies of each other, like the way Ms. Pac-Man is just Pac-Man with a bow on her head. The brother's hair was short, flopping over one eye in a swoop, but haircut aside, they could've been Tweedledum and Tweedledee.

It was <u>almost</u> funny. But instead it was creepy. They had the same flat, angry faces. The same small, accusing eyes. And the same rigid expressions as they surveyed my friends and me, obviously looking us up and down…and obviously not liking what they saw one bit.

"You're those kids who were connected to Cassidy's murder, aren't you?" the boy said at last. "I recognize you"—he jabbed a pudgy finger in Archie's face—"from the papers. You're the one who did it. Who shot him."

"I didn't shoot anyone!" Archie said, looking angry and terrified at the same time.

"Arch, calm down," Jughead said, pulling Archie back a few paces and trying to get him to chill slightly.

The last thing this moment needed was more chill, though. At least, not from me, I decided. My own rage flared up, white hot.

"Cassidy <u>broke into her house!</u>" I pointed at Veronica. "He and his friends had weapons. If she hadn't set off the alarm, god knows what they would've done to us.

"I'm not glad he's dead"—I swallowed—"but the <u>last</u> thing your friend is, is innocent. And if he weren't dead….Well, the truth is, maybe we <u>would</u> be. So it's pretty freaking hard to be sorry about that."

I paused, breathing hard. My throat felt tight and the room was too hot. Everyone was staring at me….in shock, in horror, maybe even in disgust. I hadn't just sort of, even indirectly, said I was glad someone was dead, had I? I hadn't meant it like that.

But—I had no more chill. I was a ball of anger. And maybe on some level I <u>had</u> meant it like that?

Maybe that was okay. Overdue, even.

I thought back to my reflection in the bathroom, my father's eyes glaring out of my own face. The darkness he has inside, I have it, too. I thought I had learned to accept it.

Could I accept the looks on people's faces I was seeing right now, too?

"How long you four planning to be up here, this go-round?" the sister asked, her voice toneless. "Maybe we should warn our friends. That the killers are back." The word, <u>killers</u>, rolled off her tongue in a hiss, and Archie flinched again. Jughead tightened his grip on Archie's arm. The air in the room felt like a powder keg.

Veronica took a deep breath, ready to diffuse things if possible. "I assure you, Archie's innocence <u>will</u> be proven and we'll be back out of Shadow Lake before you know it. Trust me, we're not looking to linger. We're not any happier about this than you are." Even being conciliatory, she wasn't backing down. The time for backing down had long past.

"That so?" The boy raised an eyebrow slightly, challenging.

"Unequivocally," Jughead said. "Although I'm totally digging the 'come and play with us, Danny' vibes you guys are giving off."

"Okay, then." The brother shook his head, missing <u>The Shining</u> reference—which was probably for the best—but coming to some kind of conclusion. He held out the paper bag of groceries. It rustled like wildfire, the sound making the hairs on my arms stand up. Veronica accepted it, hugging it to her chest defensively.

To the rest of us she said, "Let's go."

"Enjoy your stay," the sister called after us, the bite in her tone just skimming the surface, wrapped in a coat of plausible deniability.

But then, as the door swung shut behind us, she added—so quietly that it took a minute for the words to even register: "...and try to stay out of our way."

$$\sim\!\sim\!\sim$$

Outside the store, the moonlight was bright. Riverdale is a small town, but even our starry sky can't compare to true country. I always forget that until I'm back in real isolation again, the sky pinpricked with glittering light. Normally, it was dazzling.

Tonight, it only reminded me that the four of us were truly on our own in this, together.

"Well, I guess it shouldn't be such a surprise that we're public enemies numbers one through four in Shadow Lake, but I have to admit, that was still unnerving," Veronica said, breaking the stillness. "I guess you were right, Betty. There's no such thing as being _too_ paranoid. Now more than ever, we need to watch our backs."

"It's not paranoia if everyone really is out to get you," Jughead agreed.

"What about that scene, Jughead? Was that something out of your beloved horror canon?"

Veronica was kidding, I could tell. Trying to lighten the mood by bringing it back to our banter from earlier in the night.

"Cabin Fever." Jughead shrugged. "And don't get me started on the Grady twins in there."

It was Archie who gasped then, which was unexpected and loud enough to startle me. For a second, I thought he was laughing at Jughead's comment. But then I saw the look on his face.

"What is it, Arch?" Was he still rattled from those creepy twins? I was.

He squinted, like he was trying to make something out in the distance. "I don't know. I'm not sure."

"About what?" Veronica moved closer to him and took his hand.

"Just now. I don't know. It's late, and I'm tired, and those weirdos in there freaked me out a little, I'll admit, but..." He trailed off.

"But nothing. Tell us, Archie. We're on your side."

"This is a safe space," Jughead said, and for once he didn't sound like he was being sarcastic, either.

"I could have sworn I saw it." He turned and looked at me, his gaze steady. "A van. Just like you said, Betty. Gray. Moving slowly.

"Betty," Archie's voice shook slightly now. "I think someone _is_ watching us. Maybe even right now."

CHAPTER TWELVE

JUGHEAD

The foreboding black cat that ran us off the road, the van that may or may not have existed, that may or may not have been following us. The creepy twins who definitely had their eyes on us. The grand estate at the top of a hill (technically a lodge on the top of a mountain, but that's just semantics) . . . Everything about this road trip screamed *Turn back!* in blaring, vintage-eighties, *Stranger Things*–style font. I was trying, for everyone's sake, to maintain my typical ironic distance from the situation, but even I was feeling rattled.

And Archie—well, he wouldn't admit just how hard it had all hit him, but he'd been through the wringer this year. Starting with seeing his father shot by the Black Hood, and then going vigilante warrior with the Red Circle. All the shady stuff Hiram Lodge put him up to. Archie was milk shakes, football, and guitar. Archie wasn't cut out for this film-noir antihero existence. It was taking its toll. His eyes were tired and his mouth was set, and his hands on the steering wheel—he'd taken over the driving for the final leg of our ride—were white-knuckle tight.

I imagined us all from a Hitchcockian angle—shot from above, a camera trailing us as we wound our way up the mountainside, POV jerking from side to side to disorient the viewer, to show just how disoriented, how undone, *we* were. If I listened hard, I could imagine the soundtrack to *Psycho*—all shrieking, insistent strings—playing in the back of my brain, too.

As we wound around the mountain, the houses started to spread farther and farther apart, A-framed peaks of split-log timber soaring toward the sky, hugging against the tight cluster of evergreen forest. At the topmost point was where Lodge Lodge stood, bearing down over all of Shadow Lake—the town, but also the eponymous lake itself, pooling at the base of the valley like liquid mercury, or some kind of portal.

If only, I thought. If only it were that easy to slip out of this dimension and into a reality that was safer, more secure.

Gargoyles and . . . kings? It flashed back to me, what Pop had said when we were at the diner. About that weird role-playing game Dilton was caught up in. And Ethel, and Ben, too. Dilton had plenty of his own stuff going on; it was easy to write him off as a weirdo—even stranger and more alienated than yours truly—but right now, I could understand why he might be attracted to a game like that. Why he might want a little escapism in his life.

Hell, maybe he was onto something.

"The turn's coming up, Archiekins." Veronica still had that aggressively chipper, upbeat tone to her voice, like this trip was going to be productive—and maybe even fun!—at all costs. Even if it killed us.

Any other kids, other town, other lifetime? That would be hyperbole.

But hyperbole was a luxury we couldn't afford. Our very existence had become hyperbole.

Archie flicked the turn signal and flashed the high beams. The more isolated it got as we crawled up the mountain, the more it felt like we were driving into a void.

"Well," Veronica said, gesturing. "We've arrived in one piece."

Just barely, I thought.

To our right was the entrance to the drive, so expertly and discreetly built that we would have sped past if she hadn't pointed it out. Two trees just wider than a car's distance apart, small reflectors flashing low to the ground, and globe lights at either tree's base. What at first glance looked like more dark oblivion was actually a pebbled drive. Just past the right-side tree was a wooden post, marked only by an elaborately carved capital *L*.

Archie turned.

∿∿∿

It was cold at the top of the mountain. Even having been here before, even growing up where winters could be colder than Thanksgiving dinner at the Blossoms, it still felt like a shock, especially after the cloying, humid heat of the end of August in Riverdale. When we stepped out of the car, we shivered collectively, and when we exhaled, I swear, you could just see the trace of our breaths, little curlicues of Morse code trailing off into the atmosphere.

"I'll get the bags," Archie offered, immediately unpacking the trunk, looking like he was glad to have a concrete task, something specific to *do*. We were all feeling it—déjà vu, but real, not perceived, since yeah, we'd actually *been here before*, were still actively working, day by day, to move past the trauma of what had happened here.

No, it wasn't déjà vu; that was too euphemistic. What we had was collective PTSD. You could feel it hovering between us, humming like a third rail, as cloudy as the vapors of our breathing on the wind.

I looked at the door of the lodge—heavy, dark wood set back in an elaborate granite archway—and went cold all over. Suddenly, the last thing I wanted to do was to go inside.

Betty looped an arm through my elbow. "You ready?" she asked, reading my mind.

"Not remotely," I told her.

"I'll unlock the door, and then I have to go straight to the basement to disable the alarms and cameras," Veronica said. "It's all on a timer, so forgive me for running off. It'll just be a minute."

"*Disable* the alarms and cameras?" Archie asked, confused and maybe not totally on board with that as a plan. "Why?" He caught himself, composed himself a little more. "I mean, don't we want *some* protection, given what happened last time?"

"I hear you, Archiekins, but I wouldn't worry. The front door locks automatically. And like I said, those miscreants are locked away." Veronica seemed exceptionally confident.

Except for the one who's actually dead, I thought, but didn't say.

"They won't be back tonight. We're safe—you know that." She moved to him, tiptoeing so she could put her hands on his shoulders. "You *do* know that, right?" She kissed him, quickly but sweetly. "None of us truly *want* to be back here; I can only imagine what you must be feeling right now. Just looking around at the woods, hearing the leaves rustle, it takes me back to that night. It makes my skin crawl."

"Yeah." Archie's reply was clipped. He looked down, like he was disappointed in himself.

"But we're here with a mission, and it's going to be quick and painless. And we're completely safe up here, I promise." She turned so she was facing all of us.

"I have to disable the alarms, otherwise Daddy will be able to use the cameras to surveil us from wherever he wants, whenever he wants. And that's the last thing we need. Even if he weren't going to interfere, I would never give him the satisfaction."

"It's okay, V. If you think we're safe without the alarms, we trust you." Betty smiled—or tried to. It didn't totally reach her eyes, though. "But won't your dad notice if the systems go down?"

"Probably," Veronica admitted. "But probably not right away. That's what I'm counting on—that by the time he figures out we're up here and we've gone dark, we'll have gotten what we came for and we'll be long gone.

"It's as solid a theory as any other," I said.

Archie nodded, and wordlessly grabbed the bags again, moving to the front door more decidedly. We all followed behind. Veronica pulled a fancy leather keychain from her bag and jangled it until she found what she was looking for. It was a heavy, antique-looking brass key, like a prop from a murder mystery event. I half suppressed a laugh.

"I know," Veronica said, with a half smile of her own. "Nothing about the life of a Lodge is ever understated."

She stepped to unlock the door.

Everything happened very quickly after that. And yet it also felt like time slowed to half speed.

I felt Betty's fingers clamp into my forearm before I processed what was happening. She gripped me like a vise.

"What the hell . . ." Archie began.

That was when Veronica started to scream.

‿‿‿

Sweet Pea:

I got someone. You can relax.

PP:

No, YOU can relax. Hook me up.
We need to get this done. Send me the info.

Sweet Pea:

On it. Stay tuned.

CHAPTER THIRTEEN

VERONICA

At first, all I could hear was the piercing sound of someone's bloodcurdling scream. It felt like it was coming from everywhere, like it would never stop.

Then I realized: It was coming from *me*.

I was screaming—hysterically, like I'd completely lost my mind—and Archie had wrapped himself around me. I could smell the woodsy scent of the shampoo he used, so everyday sexy and reassuring. *Normal*. It tethered me back to the real world—just barely.

And in front of us, splayed on the doormat like the world's most gruesome welcome basket, was a pile of dead birds.

When I managed to contain myself again, to stop screaming and shaking, I forced myself to look more closely. My stomach lurched. It wasn't just birds, piled in a heap. No, they were gargantuan, evil and predatory looking, with sharp, spiky talons and wings that looked strong enough to knock a person down.

Their necks were broken.

Not just broken—*mangled*, savagely.

Their heads were twisted all the way around, and beneath the pile of carcasses, a small puddle of blood had formed— *How did we miss it? The dark, it's because it's so dark*—and was pooling along the flagstone, staining the entryway.

"What *is* that?" Betty cried, even though it was obvious, mostly because—like me, like all of us—she clearly just couldn't even believe what she was seeing with her own eyes.

"Crows, I think," Jughead said.

"No," I interjected. "They're too big for that. Aren't they too big for that?"

"They definitely are enormous," Jughead agreed. "But I'm pretty sure they're crows. Whoever left them here for us went out of their way to hand-select for size. Hopefully they were paying by unit, not by weight."

"Someone . . . left these here?" Betty's eyes were wide, her mouth severe. "But . . . who? Why? *How?*"

"Unfortunately, I don't know how we could possibly have the answers to those questions—yet," Jughead said. "But, yeah. They must have been left here on purpose. How else could this have happened? It's not the like birds themselves concocted some random Jonestown pact here. Ergo, the only possible answer is that it was a deliberate act."

"A deliberate act of *extreme* aggression," I echoed. My heart slowed back to its normal pace, and slowly, my skin cooled and that horrible sense of out-of-control terror had passed. I was regaining a modicum of composure, thank god.

My reaction had been intense. But then again, so had this little present from . . . who knew where?

"You guys, do you think it could have been those weird twins from the store?" The thought was sobering. I tried to decide if that was better or worse than having no idea where the birds came from whatsoever.

No, I decided. *Both options are equally horrifying.*

"They definitely made it clear they weren't our biggest fans," Jughead said.

"But still," Betty said, her Nancy Drew expression coming over her face. "Think about it. If it was the twins, then *when*? When did they do this? They didn't know we were in town until maybe thirty minutes ago, when we stopped in the store. They would have had to have left the store at the exact same time we did to get here and set this up. And even if they sped, that would have been cutting it pretty close. Not to mention"—she waved, indicating the mountains all around us—"it's pretty hard to speed up these roads. You can't just whip around the curves. It's too dangerous."

"Not just curvy roads. These *narrow* roads," I added. "We would have passed them, driving up. Or come up behind them, or seen them on our tail. There aren't any back roads up here. This is it. It's meant to be a private community, and *that* means security is number one. As far as I know, there's literally no way to sneak in."

"Those townies did," Jughead pointed out. "I mean, we were inside at the time, maybe not on high alert, but Andre should have seen them coming, if what you say is true. Meaning, we might not be as secure as you think."

"It's possible," I conceded. "But I still don't think the twins could have made it up here before us, on the timeline Betty's talking about." Everyone was quiet for a moment as that sunk in.

"Except . . ." Jughead sounded thoughtful.

"What, Juggie?" Betty asked.

"Except maybe we're wrong. About the timeline, I mean. It's possible that they knew we were coming up here *before* they saw us in the store. It's possible they're not working alone." His gaze darted up and around, like if he just focused hard enough, for long enough, an answer would present itself.

Betty pursed her lips, thinking. "The van." She looked excited, even though the pieces of this puzzle, once constructed, didn't paint an especially appealing picture.

Jughead nodded. "The van."

"If I was right—" Betty started pacing, caught up in her rapidly unspooling theory.

"Which, I hate to say because of the obvious and terrifying implications, it looks like you are," I said.

"Then someone—either the twins or people they're working with—well, they would have known where we were going . . . ages ago."

"Guys, that's crazy. We only, like, *just* came up with the plan to come to Shadow Lake a few hours ago." Archie's forehead creased with concern, realizing the full meaning of this.

"At Pop's," I said quietly. "An undeniably public space, no matter how much we may claim it as our own private refuge."

"The place was empty." Archie ran a hand through his hair.

"But not completely. Ben was there," Betty pointed out gently.

"He was sitting too far away to hear us talking," Archie protested.

"Maybe. But who knows? Who knows *for sure*, that is? I mean, you and I weren't even sure we saw that gray van. So maybe we can't really say. Not one hundred percent *for sure*."

"You guys," I cut in. "The van. Okay, I know I said I didn't see it. And I maintain that I didn't. But as I fully acknowledged at the time, that doesn't mean it wasn't there. Especially not if Archie saw it, too." The idea that an intruder's gaze could be focused on us even as we stood there chilled me.

"At the store," Archie said. "I said I saw it. I thought I did. I thought someone might be following us." He swallowed. "I wasn't sure, and I was hoping I was wrong."

"But given . . . this . . . *carnage*"—I stole a reluctant glance at the dead birds at the entrance, strewn like a sacrifice to some demonic darker power, shuddering—"I think we have to admit that it's a little naïve to cling to that hope."

We looked at one another. The night was still. In the distance, a bird cawed, a potent reminder of the soundless creatures that lay at our feet.

"So, what now?" Jughead asked.

I put my hands on my hips, squaring off. "Nothing changes," I said. "We have a plan, and we stick to it. We search for evidence. We find evidence. We leave with evidence. Only . . ."

"What?" Betty asked.

"Now that we know we might truly not be safe here? I suggest we do it as quickly as possible."

∧∧∧

ID UNKNOWN (1):

They just pulled up.

ID UNKNOWN (2).

Have they seen it?

ID UNKNOWN (1):

Watching now. Sending images. You can pass these along up the chain.

[1.jpg] [2.jpg] [3.jpg]

CHAPTER FOURTEEN

ARCHIE

Ronnie was right—it didn't take much to realize that. There was no way we were turning back now. And knowing that we might be in danger, that someone might be watching us *at that very moment*, all it meant was that we had to work faster, be smarter.

"The cameras?" Betty started, as Veronica went back to unlocking the door. "Are you sure—"

"I'm definitely not sure of anything, at this point." Veronica cut her off grimly. "So, maybe we don't disable *all* the surveillance. Maybe, in light of these new—and disturbing—revelations, we rethink things. I'll still have to run down to the cellar, just to turn off the alarm. If I don't enter our passcode right away, the alarm will contact the police. And we definitely *don't* want that. But while I'm down there, I'll look at the security camera setup. We can decide which ones to keep active. I'm sure we can come up with something."

Everyone nodded. "I'll come with you," I told her. "An extra set of hands—and eyes and ears—can't be a bad idea."

There was also the whole thing of how just being back at Lodge Lodge was sending visions of thugs in ski masks at me every time I blinked. I could hear it now, the sound of the townies' footsteps as they moved into the great room, baseball bats swinging, their eyes burning through the holes of their masks . . . just like the Black Hood.

Yeah. I wanted to see what kind of security system we were working with. If *anyone* was out there, watching us, I was going to catch them on film. And then I was going to catch them, period.

I was already on trial for killing Cassidy. What did I have to lose now?

"An extra set of hands would be appreciated, Archiekins. Especially if they're yours," Veronica said. "We can come back to deal with the mess once that's all taken care of."

Everyone took a deep breath—we were all trying to look braver than we were feeling, I knew—and Veronica opened the door.

⌃⌃⌃

I expected a loud blaring, or a beep, or something to tell us that the alarm had been triggered. But inside the Lodge, everything looked perfect and peaceful, like nothing violent had ever happened here. Obviously the place wouldn't still be messed up after the home invasion—I mean, the Lodges definitely had some fancy cleaning crew coming on a regular basis. But it still creeped me out more than I wanted to admit—even to myself—how totally innocent and serene it all appeared on the surface.

"Archie, are you coming?" Veronica's voice broke me out of my trance.

"Right behind you." I snapped to attention. *No time for spacing out.*

Game on.

∧∧∧

I hadn't been down to the cellar with Veronica last time we were here. Just that word, *cellar*, made me think of Jughead's horror movies—bare lightbulbs swinging from strings, dirt floors, little windowless crawl spaces. But even a Lodge basement was a little more high-end than normal people's. Of course, the basement was finished, and I followed Veronica down a set of stone stairs that mimicked the archway and the great room fireplace.

It was dark down there, even with Veronica flicking light switches along the way, but as things lit up, I could see walls paneled in dark, expensive wood. I had a minute of appreciating the craftsmanship of the building—after all that time working for Andrews Construction, I really was my dad's son, and I had learned a thing or two. But it was only a minute. I needed to be strong—for Veronica, for all of us—but I didn't *feel* strong, not really. Every dark, shadowy corner was possibly hiding an intruder; every creak of a floorboard could mean we weren't alone.

I wasn't afraid of the dark. Never was, not even when I was a little kid. But there were so many other things in this world to be afraid of. And we all had firsthand knowledge of so much of it.

"It's a silent alarm, Archie," Veronica said, like maybe she'd noticed I was confused by how quiet and still the house was. "But it's on a timer. And we have maybe two minutes to spare."

She jiggled a doorknob I hadn't noticed, then banged the door open with her hip. "In here," she said, beckoning me. "The keypad is just above the safe."

I heard the click of a lamp, and one corner of the room glowed yellow. I blinked, trying to adjust my eyes to the light.

I blinked again, this time with surprise. The room was obviously Hiram's office. It was like a smaller, cabin-style knockoff of his office at the Pembrooke: a large, solid, heavy-looking wood desk against the back wall, a swooping leather wingback chair, a plush animal-skin rug splayed on the floor. Behind his desk, where at the Pembrooke, the oil portrait of

Veronica hung, was an immense stuffed moose head, antlers reaching, branching wider than the span of a car's bumper. Its eyes were glazed, but it still looked like it was watching us . . . and it didn't like what it saw.

"Do you know the code? What if it rotates, or something?" There were too many variables to this plan. Too many things could go wrong.

"I know the code," Veronica said confidently. She jabbed a polished finger at the keypad in quick little taps. "It doesn't rotate. It's always my birthday." She finished tapping.

A little flashing light went red.

"That doesn't look great." *Crap.* It didn't rotate—except when it did.

Veronica frowned. "Shush. I must have mis-entered a number. I thought my nerves were steady, but I guess none of us are completely immune to the psychological fallout of such a high-stakes scenario." She leaned in and peered more intently at the pad, pressing a series of numbers again.

We both held our breath as she finished and moved back.

It turned green. Veronica squealed. "I don't want to say 'I told you so . . .'"

I grabbed her and swept a lock of hair out of her eyes. "You definitely told me so."

She kissed me and leaned her head against my chest. I breathed in the nearness of her. "Crisis averted," she said. Her voice was slightly muffled from being pressed against me. "Let this be a harbinger."

I stiffened. It was too hard to hear the word *harbinger* without my brain auto-completing the phrase *harbinger of doom*.

That's when the lights went out.

∧∧∧

If I'd had a momentary twitch when Veronica said *harbinger*, the sudden darkness pushed me over the edge. I grabbed Veronica tightly—too tightly, it was reflexive; I was freaked out—and pulled her in even closer than she'd been.

"Always my white knight," she said, running a free hand in small circles between my shoulder blades. "I think we all must have a little post-traumatic stress disorder, being back at the literal scene of the crime, but it must be most acute for you."

"I'm fine," I said, gruff.

"Maybe that's true"—her lips found mine again, taking me by surprise in the dark—"but it doesn't have to be. Archie, I love that you're so determined to protect us all. And you can be strong—for us, for yourself—if that's how you're feeling, if that's what you want. But you don't have to be strong to the exclusion of any other emotion. What happened to us was scary. And messy. And now we're reliving some of it. And it's okay if that feels scary. And messy."

And just like that—just when I'd thought I couldn't possibly love her more—I realized how right she was, how amazing and smart she was, and how lucky *I* was to have her in my corner.

"I would be feeling a little better if it weren't pitch-black down here," I admitted. "It's not even storming or anything. What's going on?"

I could actually feel her shoulders scrunch up in a shrug, against me. "We're so far up in the mountains," she explained. "No matter how much a person pays—and believe me, Daddy spared no expense—electricity, internet, all the wiring can sometimes be a little touch and go. The good news—"

So there was a "good news" in this whole situation. It wasn't as reassuring as I would have liked.

"—is that Daddy, like any good homesteader, prepared for this eventuality. We're hooked up to a backup generator that will engage automatically. We just have to wait a few minutes."

She took my hand and led me to a small leather sofa in one corner. "We may as well get comfortable," she said. "After all, even when the power comes back on, we may have a long night ahead of ourselves."

∿∿∿

We sat like that, side by side in the dark, for a few minutes. I listened to the rise and fall of Ronnie's breath, the steady rhythm of her inhales and exhales. "Do you think Betty and Jug are okay?" I asked finally.

"They're probably a little nonplussed," she said. "But unfortunately, until the generator kicks in, they can't get down here to us. The door to the cellar locks automatically in the event of a power outage lasting more than a couple of minutes."

"Why?"

"It creates a sort of makeshift panic room," she said. She paused. "I know. It's weird. Chalk it up to good old-fashioned one-percenter paranoia. It's a thing."

I laughed. "I wouldn't know."

"But you laughed!" She gave me a playful tap. "You've been so serious."

"I've been in a weird mood since the party," I admitted. "I'm sorry. I should've worked harder to snap out of it. It's not fair to you."

"That's sweet of you to say. But first off, I can take care of myself," she said. "And second of all . . . I wasn't just talking about tonight, after the party. I meant over the summer. Ever since the student council elections. Since . . ." She hesitated.

"Since my arrest," I finished.

"Don't get me wrong, it's completely valid. I told you, you're allowed to have feelings, you *should* have feelings, and I meant what I said. But I hate seeing you like this. I hate that it's my fault."

"It's *not* your fault," I insisted. Every time she said something like that, I felt it, like a stab in my gut.

"It's *my* father. Who wouldn't have a bone to pick with you if you'd never gotten involved with me. Whether or not I was an active participant in your downfall, it's safe to say it boils down to us getting together in the first place."

"We don't know that for sure," I pointed out. "Your father does have *lots* of bones to pick with *lots* of people. There's no guarantee that he wouldn't have gotten around to me sooner or later, even if you and I weren't dating."

We both laughed at the sad reality of that. What else was there to do?

"It does have a certain Shakespearean quality to it. An inevitability," Ronnie admitted. She ran her fingers up the inside of my arm. "But, I'm not sorry we *are* together." She paused and then went on in a slightly unsure tone, something I wasn't accustomed to from someone as fearless as Veronica. "Are you?"

"God, Ronnie, of course not." I hugged her to me. "You have to know, no matter what happens, or how this shakes out, I love you. Completely. Nothing will change that. There's nothing that could ever possibly make me regret finding you. I don't even want to think about what would have happened if I *hadn't*. This was meant to be." Ugh, so cheesy. But I had to be real with her.

"Good," she said. "Because the feeling is completely mutual."

My entire body flooded with feeling for her. God, I loved her so much. I grabbed her and kissed her, first softly, our lips brushing together and her hair swinging gently against my cheeks. Then more urgently, like there was no way to get as close to her as I wanted to be.

For a few minutes, we didn't talk anymore.

∿∿∿

"I hope Betty and Jug aren't too freaked out."

"Well, I'll admit, this little blackout has gone on a touch longer than I expected, but I still maintain it's a brief, temporary blip on the radar. I'm sure those two can entertain themselves." A devilish smile crept into Ronnie's voice. "We did."

I laughed. "Maybe it's not the end of the world if the power stays down a little bit longer." We definitely found some ways to kill the time.

Ronnie laughed, too. "Hear, hear."

After a minute, though, her tone got serious again. Wistful.

"Archiekins," she started. "I'm glad we're here, and we can laugh about this whole sordid mess. Like I said, you deserve that and more. But . . . you know, I know why you were so triggered by Reggie's silly, tasteless comments. Of course, you have nothing to be worried about. But I understand exactly why he got under your skin."

I sighed. "I don't mean to be the jealous boyfriend. I don't want to be that guy. And it's not that I don't trust you," I insisted. "But Reggie and I . . . we've always been rivals. I don't even know when it first started, that's how much it's just become, like, a part of our dynamic. Our thing. And he's had an eye on you since your first day at Riverdale High. All the guys have. Not that I blame them."

"And, if I were an object to be pursued and attained, I'd be flattered," she said. "But as it is, I'm a strong woman with independent thoughts who is capable of self-direction."

"He's sneaky."

"He's a complete snake," she agreed. "Some of the pranks he's pulled since I got here have been staggering in their complexity. Which I'm sure factors heavily into your current anxiety. That time he convinced us all he was *dying*? To get Josie to go with him to homecoming? Diabolical. And deranged. But the key here is *Josie*. She's the one he's always trying to get to. Not me. No matter what he said to you tonight. That was just Reggie being . . . Reggie."

"Still," I pointed out. "There's always collateral."

She was silent, thinking. She couldn't exactly argue the point.

Bringing up Josie wasn't exactly the best way to convince me he was harmless. If Reggie hadn't been so hell-bent on getting Josie to go out with him, he and Ronnie wouldn't have . . .

Ugh. I hated to even think about it. But since he'd gotten all in my face at his party, I couldn't push the memory out of my mind.

The thing was, even *after* the whole crazy "dying wish" prank Reggie pulled last year, Josie hadn't *completely* written him off. Maybe she didn't want to be his girlfriend, but she definitely had some complicated feelings for him. Feelings that involved enjoying his feelings for *her*. And entertaining them *just enough*, once in a while. To keep him coming back for more. Not in a cruel way, not really. Just in the way that someone who's conflicted might behave.

So it was our winter school play, a production of *The Crucible*. (Since what Riverdale High needed was any excuse for a witch hunt.) The drama club was ready, the sets were built, everyone was off-book and getting psyched for opening night.

Then came the plague.

I'm sort of kidding. It wasn't, like, the Black Death or anything—though in Riverdale, you'd definitely be forgiven for making that assumption. But it was messy and tricky and it ground production down to a halt, anyway.

Mononucleosis. "The Kissing Disease." And it seemed like *everyone* was infected.

Eventually, we'd all be affected, too.

It started with a school-wide announcement. We were in dress rehearsal, and it was two days before opening night.

One by one, we'd started to notice absences in classes. A stray cough or two, and the next day, someone's seat would be empty. So I guess it wasn't a total surprise when Weatherbee's voice crackled over the intercom.

"Hello. This is your principal with a message for the entire Riverdale High School community. I'm here to announce a potential outbreak of mononucleosis, commonly known as 'the Kissing Disease.'"

Backstage, all the crew members snickered.

"All students are to be examined by Nurse Shapely—"

More snickering.

"—and any student confirmed to be carrying the virus will be quarantined in the gym until dismissal."

All the laughing stopped, like a car slamming on the brakes. *Quarantined?*

But Weatherbee wasn't done. There was one last sucker punch waiting for us. "Until further notice, all after-school activities are suspended. Thank you."

Cheryl was the first to lose it. "This is outrageous!" she shouted. She stormed down to Shapely's office with the rest of us for her examination.

And like the rest of us, the results were swift, and damning. Positive. Positive tests all the way down.

Into the gym we went. It had been converted into a weird little holding pen for the infected, cots everywhere and electric tea kettles for . . . I don't know, boiling water for tea, or maybe for sanitizing stuff. It was like being in a war movie, but more surreal—half the patients were still in their *Crucible* period costumes, including Cheryl. Who, as we all know, was never one to pass up the chance to shove some extra drama into a scenario.

"Let me out of here!" she screamed, banging on the heavy double doors.

From the corner, Jughead coughed. It was small, but Cheryl caught it, of course. "J'accuse!" she shouted. Jughead just looked confused. He glanced at Cheryl, questioning.

"Cheryl, relax," Jug said. "It's been an hour."

"Excuse me, human smallpox blanket," she said, looming over him threateningly. "Because of *you*, our production is getting canceled. You've contaminated all of us with your 'Bughead' germs." She jabbed a razor-sharp, bloodred-painted pointer finger at Betty, who was seated next to him on his cot, an arm slung around him.

"It makes me sick. Sick!" Cheryl spat, and I could see Jug fighting the urge to point out that in fact, she *was* sick, there was no 'making' anymore, it was just, like, her state of being. "To think I had to *kiss* your thin, chapped lips during rehearsals.

Ugh." She pulled a lip gloss out of the apron of her costume and slathered it on.

"Cheryl—" Josie rushed over. "That's *my* lip gloss."

Cheryl dropped the tube to the ground like it was radioactive.

Jughead laughed. "See? You've been sharing Josie's lip stuff all this time. Maybe you're the one who got *me* sick!"

I don't think he really meant it or even cared that much—he was sick, and with Jug, what's done is done, no sense crying over spilled infectious disease germs—but it *was* a little funny watching Cheryl get amped up.

Her eyes practically glittered with rage. She stood in a power posture, legs apart, hands on hips. "That's it," she snapped. "We're getting to the bottom of who this mono patient zero is, and we're going to eradicate this fiend from our cast. Because the show, as they say, must go on."

"Sounds like you're instigating a witch hunt," Jug said, making an obvious reference to the play itself.

If Cheryl saw the irony, she wasn't amused. "Exactly."

∿∿∿

No one was immune to Cheryl's wrath. She pulled her beloved Josie into a corner and faced off against her. "Josephine McCoy, who have you been kissing?" she demanded.

(This was before the days of #Choni, and none of us realized at the time that Cheryl may have had a special interest in Josie's love life.)

"No one," Josie said, looking equally annoyed and worried. If anyone could handle Cheryl at her most Bombshell, it was Josie, but this was . . . intense.

Cheryl wasn't buying it. "No rugged roadies? No secret showmances?"

"I haven't been with anyone," Josie insisted—but her voice shook slightly.

Veronica, Reggie, and I were watching from the sidelines, as surreptitiously as we could. I couldn't help but react to Josie's response. "That's not true," I whispered to Veronica.

But I guess I didn't whisper as quietly as I'd meant to.

Cheryl whirled to me, focusing that rage in my direction. "Do you have something to say, Archie?" she demanded.

Reggie jabbed a finger in my side. "Shut it, Andrews," he warned.

"It's nothing," I said, glancing from Cheryl to Reggie, both of whom looked totally ready to split my skull if I didn't heed their orders, stat.

"Spill it!" Cheryl shouted. For a second there, she seemed like a bigger threat than Reggie.

I swallowed. "It's just . . . I saw Josie and Reggie. In the music room." I would still go in there sometimes, to practice guitar and work on my songs, even if music was taking a backseat to other stuff. *Usually* the room was empty. But not that day. "They were alone," I said, ignoring Reggie's insistent looks. "But, together."

Josie glanced at the floor, avoiding Cheryl's accusing gaze. For Cheryl, that was probably more damning than if she'd just straight-up confessed.

Now Cheryl looked *truly* sick. Her skin went from "pale" to "pallid," and beads of sweat broke out on her forehead. "Reggie Mantle?" she asked Josie. Her voice almost cracked. She made a face, then pulled herself together.

"You see what happens when you go slumming with a gutter-mouth like Mantle?" she snapped. "He's like Pop Tate's cheese fries—a tasty snack, but one that leaves you feeling sick."

And Josie *did* look sick—beyond the fact that she had mono. "We were trying to keep it on the DL."

"Oh, I bet." Cheryl sneered.

Josie stood, looking shaky. "I need some fresh air. And a lozenge."

Reggie glared at me. "I'm not done with you, Andrews," he promised. But he moved to Josie and took her arm. "Babe, wait. Can we talk?"

"I have to call Val and tell her I'm sick," she said. She fumbled with her phone, stabbing at it in frustration. "We have to cancel our gig this weekend—"

"Look," Reggie cut in. "I'm sorry it's so embarrassing for you to be with me."

Josie clenched her hand around her phone and dropped it to her side. "*That's* why you think I'm upset?" Her eyes went dark. "Because people found out about us? No, no, no . . ." She shook her head, like she couldn't decide if she was amused or disgusted. "It's because every time I let my guard down with you, Mantle, you let me down. It's always something. I don't know why I don't learn my lesson."

"Okay, there was that prank," Reggie rushed in. "That wasn't cool, I know, but it was just because you make me crazy, I *had* to go to homecoming with you—" He was babbling, and sweating, too. I wasn't used to seeing Mantle looking so flustered.

Honestly, maybe this makes me a bad person, but it wasn't the worst.

"I'm upset because if I got mono from you, it means you've been kissing other people. It must be one of these walking dead." She swept her hand across the gym, indicating the rows of cots covered in shivering students. "Who was it? Becky with the good hair?"

Reggie flinched. "I swear, I haven't been with anyone but you."

"Uh-huh," she said, unconvinced. "Then how'd we both end up with mono? *I* haven't been stepping out. Now, because of you, I have to cancel paid performances."

"But—"

Josie cut him off. "It's fine," she said. "We had fun. But I only have the bandwidth for one thing—and that's being a star. Real talk: We both know I can't be attached right now. You understand." The look she gave him was pure ice.

Josie stalked off, phone in hand, not bothering to throw even a last glance at Reggie in her wake. He cracked his knuckles, looking like he was planning to run after her, but Cheryl wasn't done with him.

"Hold on, lover boy." She grabbed him by the shoulders and shoved him down in a folding chair. It scraped against the wood of the gym floor, loud and awkward. "Let's discuss."

"What, Cheryl?" Reggie sighed. "Just get it over with."

"Rumor is Jen Clancy showed you a pretty good backhand on the tennis court," she said. Her eyebrows were angry slashes and her cheekbones looked sharp enough to cut glass.

"That was a lie she started to get back at her ex," Reggie protested.

"What about you and Donna Foley in the AV room?" Cheryl countered.

"Ha! She wishes. And I've never even been in the AV room," he said. "I'm allergic to nerds."

"Kelly Thompson?"

Reggie made an incredulous face. "*You* started that rumor after she made fun of your dry elbows!"

"My elbows are *not* on trial here!" Cheryl shouted. "You are going to tell me who you've been kissing!"

Jughead, Betty, Ronnie, and I had formed a small huddle next to the showdown. We couldn't help ourselves.

"Should we stop this?" Betty asked.

"Are you crazy?" Veronica said. "This is like chocolate without the calories. Heaven."

Meanwhile, I had concerns of my own. "Do you think Reggie's going to kick my ass for outing him and Josie?" I asked Jughead.

"Reggie loves a good fight," he pointed out, rubbing the back of his neck. "So I'd say it's inevitable."

"How many times do I have to tell you?" Reggie was saying, his hands up in the air now. "I've only been with Josie! Ever since we made out in the laundry room at Kevin's costume party."

Veronica started, her eyes going wide. She gasped and clapped a hand over her mouth. "Laundry room?" she muttered. "Oh no . . ."

"Ronnie, what is it?" I asked, my stomach turning with suspicion.

"I think I'm going to be sick." She did look pale.

"You already are. With mono," Cheryl reminded her. She shooed Reggie from the folding chair. "Reggie, move. You're excused, for the time being. Don't go far. But that hot seat now belongs to Veronica."

Veronica collapsed into the chair, looking shaky.

"This is no time for your gothic heroine fainting," Cheryl said. "Muster your strength and spill it, Typhoid Mary."

Veronica sighed, looking truly sick to her stomach. I couldn't tell whether it was from the mono or from whatever memory she was searching for, but either way, I was having sympathy pains of my own. I didn't like where this was going—there was no way it was going to be a story with a happy ending, given where we all were right now.

"I mean, you all remember that party," she started, speaking quietly. "It was just after everyone had been cast. Kevin invited us all over as sort of an icebreaker. A meet and greet."

Betty nodded, recalling. "Since he was the director, he'd pilfered the entire theater department's costume shop."

"And Reggie and I were both wearing—"

"Yes," Veronica said, knowing where I was going with it before the words even came out of my mouth. "As luck would have it, the two of you both found yourselves dressed as Romeo." She forced a half smile. "In Reggie's case, the statement seemed ironic. Especially when he tried to woo Josie while sending understudies to refill his drink."

"Right. 'Some Romeo you are,' she said to him. She was not impressed."

"'And some Juliet you could be. If you'd just give me a chance,'" Cheryl quoted. She had been watching them, too, that night.

"We were standing close enough to Josie and Reggie that we couldn't help overhearing their conversation," Veronica went on. "Then we were interrupted by Kevin. 'No alcohol in those drinks, right guys? My dad is just upstairs.' I told him of course not. And I don't think there was any, at that point, anyway. He excused himself to go tell Dilton to turn the music down.

"Well, not to be too scandalous, but the soiree was feeling fairly sedate and I was in the mood for some fun. So I whispered to Archie to meet me in the laundry room in five minutes."

"And you agreed, I assume," Cheryl said. I nodded. "Men are such testosterone-fueled beasts." She sniffed.

"It was Ronnie's idea!" I said. Not that I owed Cheryl Blossom an explanation—or an apology—for stealing a few minutes with my girl.

"And doesn't that make you the lucky Neanderthal at her side?" Cheryl quipped. "Meanwhile, I had a front row seat to Moose bringing the drinks back for Reggie and Josie—don't even ask me how Reggie Mantle managed to get Moose to do his bidding. But it backfired, anyway, because when you combine someone with all the grace and poise associated with the name *Moose* with an overfilled Solo cup, sartorial disaster is inevitable. He tripped, and doused Josie.

"Of course, dear worrywart director Kevin Keller took note of this tumble and took the opportunity to revel in the angst of it all. 'We have to get this shirt cleaned immediately, or my directing career is going to be over before it began.' He was simply simpering."

"The costumes," Betty said. "No wonder he was freaking out."

"You can't imagine the degree of understatement, dear cousin," Cheryl said. "Kevin whisked Josie to the bathroom."

"And meanwhile, I was idling patiently in the laundry room, waiting on Archie," Veronica said.

My head started spinning as I put it all together.

She bit her lip. "I should have realized. Archie, I should have recognized his voice, or realized it wasn't *your* voice. But the party was loud and I had no cause for suspicion; I was only eagerly awaiting your arrival. So when there was a knock on the door, and someone said, 'My fair Juliet, are you in there?' . . ."

"You assumed it was me," I finished. My brain had already filled in the blanks. My stomach felt like I'd swallowed a fistful of needles. "Meanwhile, I was upstairs, knocking on the bathroom door, trying to see if someone could tell me where the laundry room was. But Kevin was too busy with Josie trying to clean off her costume."

"Wait a minute." If Reggie's brain was slower than mine to get the memo, he was definitely more excited than I was about it. "Wait. Wait." He started laughing. "So, let me get this straight: When I thought I was kissing Josie, it was actually *Veronica*?" He doubled over, collapsing with hysterical laughter. Josie, off in a corner of the quarantine space, looked less amused.

"I'm so sorry, Archiekins," Veronica said, looking truly devastated. "I can't believe I didn't realize. I have no excuse. It just . . . it never would have occurred to me that something like that could even happen."

If Ronnie was devastated, they didn't have a word for what I was feeling. The idea of Reggie kissing Veronica made me want to go Red Circle vigilante again, or worse. The only thing that stopped me was Veronica's obvious misery—it had been a total accident, she felt terrible, and I couldn't stand to make it worse for her.

"Bro!" Reggie crowed. "Just call me 'Mister Steal Your Girl!'" He pumped his fists in the air, prompting another wave of rage to wash over me. Betty put a hand on my back to calm me.

"Catchy," Jughead said. "It has a real non-ring to it. Definitely something to be super proud of."

Betty stepped forward. "Enough, Cheryl! This is over. All you've caused is pain and suffering. And we're no closer to finding out who patient zero is." She took a deep breath. "We were all drinking out of that punch bowl at Kevin's that night. If anyone was sick, then we're *all* sick."

"Betty's right," Jughead said. "I don't think there's any way to know who started it."

I sagged with the weight of that information. All that anger and insecurity that Cheryl had dredged up, imagining Reggie and Veronica, arms locked around each other . . . Even if it was a complete accident, even if she had no idea, the whole thing made me queasy and furious.

And we still didn't even know who'd caused the outbreak. So what was the point, other than to open the floodgates on one of my all-time worst fears?

We were standing there, considering everything that had come out and how totally in the dark we all still were, when the intercom crackled with another message from Weatherbee.

"Hello, this is Principal Weatherbee with an announcement," we heard, his voice loud and echoing throughout the gym. "I'm pleased to say that today's outbreak has been contained. We will resume with our regularly scheduled school activities, including tonight's production of *The Crucible*. Thank you."

The room went still as the intercom cut out.

"The play is back on?" I hadn't even seen Josie creep closer to our little cluster.

"How is that possible?" Cheryl demanded.

Betty stepped forward. "The understudies," she hissed.

She reached out to Cheryl, who was busy taking selfies with Josie. Her emotional turnaround could give you whiplash. "Smile! Hashtag survivors."

"Cheryl, I need to see your phone. I think I know who got us all sick."

∧∧∧

And in the end, it *was* our resident Nancy Drew who cracked the case. Scrolling through Cheryl's photo album, she realized: The understudies had sabotaged us. It was the only explanation that made sense. We were using red cups. They were drinking from blue cups. As Betty put it, "It was an orchestrated attack."

They had a million reasons to be fed up, the understudies. Underdogs, so much of the time. Midge, always at the bottom of the Vixens' pyramid. Moose, forever the butt of Reggie's jokes and pranks. Ethel, whose *Blue and Gold* stories got bumped anytime Betty and Jughead thought they had the hotter scoop.

Yeah, they had the motive. When you stacked all their possible motives together, I was surprised they hadn't planned something like this sooner.

But really, at that point, the mono was the last thing on my mind. Swollen glands, exhaustion . . . quarantine. Fine. I could deal with all of that. But Reggie and Veronica making out, even inadvertently? *That* was an image that would haunt me.

And there was nothing anyone could do to rewind that moment or take it away. It was in the past. It was done. It was one of my worst fears, and now it was real.

∧∧∧

So, considering our history, it made sense that I'd be a little sensitive to Reggie flirting with Ronnie, or making any off hand comments about going after her. The thing was, Reggie knew that Ronnie was my kryptonite, and he was goading me on purpose. The last thing I needed to do was to let him get under my skin. But I was human; obviously I made mistakes. I had reactions. And when everything else was falling apart, the last thing I could handle was the idea that my relationship with Veronica—the best thing in my life—was going to be threatened. While I was locked up, in prison. And couldn't do anything. About that, or anything else.

"Archiekins, that accidental lip-lock with Reggie Mantle was beyond unfortunate," Veronica said. "And of course, it would bother you that he's dangling the possibility of an encore in your face." She took my hand and kissed it. "But you have nothing to worry about. If *anything* positive can be said to have come from that extreme *pas de deux faux pas*, it's that I will forever and beyond be able to pick your pucker out of a lineup. I promise."

"I know, Ronnie." I meant it. "And I promise, I'll let it go. These are—"

"These are harrowing times," she filled in. "I get it. Your brief indulgence in chivalrous semi-hysteria is completely understandable. But I'm Team Varchie all the way."

Her lips met mine in the dark, making promises stronger than words.

But before we could get too comfortable, again, the lights flipped back on.

Veronica smiled at me, brushing a curl back behind one ear. "No rest for the weary, my one true Romeo," she said. "Back to work."

CHAPTER FIFTEEN

BETTY

Dear Diary:

Since Jason Blossom's death, my friends and I have dealt with <u>way</u> creepier things than a stupid power outage. So when the lights went out, Jug and I had no trouble keeping our cool. It took maybe a minute for us to realize what had happened.

"It's the mountains," Jughead said. "True <u>Deliverance</u> country. No matter how much money you pour into a place's infrastructure, it's going to be dicey when the wind blows in the wrong direction or the temperature drops a fraction of a percentage."

"It's <u>Hiram Lodge,</u>" I said. "Even if he can't ensure nonstop Wi-Fi, I'm sure he has some über-generator in the basement fired up and ready to go for just such occasions."

"In the meantime…" Suddenly, Jug's face lit up, a glow rising from under his chin as he waved his phone flashlight at me.

"Don't waste your batteries," I scolded. "Just in case this takes longer than we expect."

He took my hand. "I'll turn it off as soon as we get downstairs to see how Veronica and Archie are doing. Hopefully they managed to disable the alarm before the power went out."

"I feel like if the alarm hadn't been disabled, we'd know by now. Outage or no."

I let Jug lead me down the hall, padding quietly over thick woven rugs in deep earth tones. "I'm having flashbacks to that time we watched <u>Wait Until Dark</u> at the Twilight on Terror Tuesday."

"Please, Jug," I begged. "Like this isn't creepy enough without your references?"

"Fair," he conceded.

The main floor of the lodge was enormous: an airy, open-plan space with a chef's kitchen overlooking an island that led to a long, solid dining table. Beyond that were cozy couches and overstuffed chairs and an enormous stone hearth fireplace flanked by two bins of fresh-cut firewood. A widow's walk ran the length of the upstairs, where the bedroom suites were, but other than that, the hallway to the basement was one of the only small, narrow spaces in the whole house.

And it <u>felt</u> small, tight, claustrophobic, even though it was still probably almost as wide as a Riverdale High hallway. Or maybe that was just a slow creep of dread coming over me, no matter how much I tried to tell myself that I wasn't afraid of something as banal as the dark, that I'd stared the Black Hood down in cold blood and recognized that blood as my own.

The farther we crept down the hall, lit by only the soft white of Jughead's phone, the harder it was to cling to that shred of bravado.

"It feels like we're marching the Green Mile," I said. I was trying to joke, but it fell flat in the eerily quiet shadows of the blackout, especially on the heels of my admonishment about Jug's horror reference.

"There definitely is a certain Dead Man Walking quality to this hallway. Like the door at the end of it will undoubtedly be marked room 237. Or 1408." Two of his favorite Stephen King references. "Sorry, we weren't supposed to be thinking about horror movies."

"It's okay," I said. "I like your creepy hobbies, even if I'm being a scaredy-cat right now. Maybe it just means we're a perfect match?"

"I definitely support that interpretation. But—wait—look." He shone his light.

It was a door: dark, heavy wood, like all of them, all the surfaces in this place, gleaming of expensive polish and smelling musky with age in a way that was reassuring. And planted staunchly between us and wherever Veronica and Archie were right now. "A little bit imposing, I'll give you that," Jughead said. "But it's definitely not room 237. So we don't have to panic just yet."

He reached out for the door handle, gave it a rattle. Nothing—not even a wiggle.

"Can I panic now?" I asked. Again, teasing, and again, falling flat.

Jug tugged at the edge of his crown beanie, shaking free one wild lock of hair. Suddenly, realization dawned on his adorable face. "It's a panic room!"

"There's a panic room in the basement?"

"No. Well, yes. Sort of." He shook his head. "Sorry. What I mean is that I'm pretty sure the entire basement functions like a panic room. Work with me here. It would make sense. Hiram Lodge is insanely rich. Insanely rich people are often <u>also</u> insanely paranoid, and that leads to insanely convoluted, complicated, high-end home security systems. My best guess is the basement door is set to lock when the power cuts out."

"What if you're on the wrong side of the door when that happens, though?" This panic room seemed to have a few flaws in its system.

Jughead shrugged. "I'm sure there's a code that the Lodges know. Like an override, if that happens. But, we're not Lodges. Veronica wasn't expecting an outage, and Hiram Lodge isn't expecting us here, at all, in the first place. So, no override."

"Should we call to them?" Would they even hear us? This place was charming and cozy, but I knew looks could be deceiving; it was built like a fortress. Hiram Lodge was a man who would leave nothing to chance.

"We can try." He banged on the door and shouted, "Archie! Veronica!" a few times. "It's probably soundproofed." As if to confirm what he was saying, his banging and shouting was met with stony silence and the sound of our own cautious breathing.

There was such a thing as <u>too</u> much peace and quiet, I decided.

"Why do you know so much about rich people and their safe houses, anyway?" I asked, slightly charmed by this most recent peek under the curtain of Mr. Jughead Jones's psyche, despite the circumstances.

"Hiram Lodge is basically Bruce Wayne, like if Bruce Wayne were evil, right?" He laughed. "Maybe Lex Luthor."

"Don't let Veronica hear you say that," I warned. "Even though she agrees."

∧∧∧

The lights weren't down for that long, really—maybe twenty minutes? At first, I was staring at my phone, watching the minutes tick by. But after five or so had passed in relative peace, Jug slid down the edge of the wall until he was crouched just outside the door to the basement. I lowered and stretched out next to him, legs tucked up under my chin and me tucked up under his arm. I guess it would have made more sense to go back to the great room, which was made for lounging. But it was dark, and all we had for flashlights were our phones, and I think neither of us wanted to risk running out of battery before the generator kicked in.

Anyway, for whatever dumb, superstitious, unspoken reason, we didn't want to stray too far from the basement door, like it was super important to be <u>right there</u> when the lights went on and it popped open again.

Jughead laughed, reminding me exactly how stock-still everything was by breaking the silence.

"What?" I asked, though I couldn't help but grin just to hear him chuckle.

"Betty Cooper," he said, twisting the tip of my ponytail around one hand. "I bet this wasn't what you had in mind when you agreed to be my Serpent Queen."

I thought about it, and then I laughed, too. "Honestly? I don't think I had _anything_ specific in mind when you first asked. It's hard to do too much advance prep for something like that."

"Yeah, it's definitely a role you have to just lean into. Blind faith," he agreed. "It's been that way for me, with the Serpents, anyway." He stifled a yawn, reminding me what a long day it had been for all of us. "If you had asked me when we were little if the two of us would end up together? I would've thought you were crazy."

"Hey!" I elbowed him.

"No, I mean, I would've been _thrilled_ at the idea that _the_ Betty Cooper would be interested in, well, _Jughead Jones._"

I understood what he meant, and for once it felt like we were just having an honest conversation about who we were, to ourselves and to each other, and the specter of Archie Andrews, Boy Wonder Next Door, was nowhere to be seen.

"And now, here we are—"

"—madly in love," I teased, in an uncharacteristically mushy moment.

"Madly in love," he agreed, hugging me closer to him. "...on another one of our stakeout/manhunt/investigation/weirdest dates ever. And I wouldn't have it any other way."

"Me either." I rested my head against his chest, taking in the worn-leather smell of his Serpents jacket. It smelled like home to me.

Still, though, maybe it was the...darkness in me, whatever it is that keeps me from truly being that "perfect Betty Cooper" that everyone expects...but I had to ask. "Jughead...What do you think will happen if Archie <u>is</u> convicted?"

He shrugged. "I don't know, really. I mean, how could we? I know what it was like when my dad was in jail, which...wasn't great. I mean, in addition to just straight-up missing him, there's also that extra layer of being worried. Is he doing okay? Is he eating? Is he safe? Is he being honest with me when I ask? And of course—the answer is always no. My dad never wanted to worry me."

"Archie will be the same way..." I mused, then realized what I'd said. "I mean—I don't think he's going to be convicted, I just meant—"

"—I know what you meant, Betty. Don't worry." He sighed. "And yeah. Archie <u>would</u> be exactly the same way."

"We can't let him go, Jughead." FP was tough, and Jughead had still worried about him in jail, naturally. Archie was <u>strong</u>, sure, but he wasn't <u>tough</u>. In prison, they'd chew him up and spit him out before breakfast.

"I know," he said, putting a warm, comforting palm on the back of my neck. "We're going to do everything we can to prevent it."

He kissed me gently on the top of my head, making me smile again. "You definitely just got a mouthful of ponytail, there."

"Maybe." He laughed.

"Sorry about the hairspray."

We sat in the quiet, both of us trying not to think about what might happen if Archie went away. Trying instead to reminisce about everything we'd been through since Veronica arrived, the end of last summer, the month when everything changed.

Jughead settled back against the wall again. "Hey, do you remember that little weekend trip we took to the city with Veronica last year? When she was still the new girl but our whole, 'core four,' four-way best friendship had already been sealed?"

"Of course."

There were so many amazing aspects of that trip to remember...but there was also an underlying uneasiness that had come over us during our time there. Some stuff that had come to the surface. Call it the Riverdale Effect. Most of the time, I tried not to think about any of that. I tried to focus on the good.

Most of the time, it worked.

∿∿∿

Veronica had invited us out of town for our *first* weekend getaway. And while there was drama, sure, it was nothing like that original weekend at Shadow Lake. Small mercies, etc.

She told us we were going to meet some old friends of hers, first at their place, and then head to dinner. Archie was adorable— staring, wide-eyed, at the skyscrapers and neon lights, the billboards, the yellow cabs. He was acting like an excited puppy. In the elevator to V's friend's place, he counted the floors as we ascended. "Fifty-five, fifty-six, fifty-seven . . ."

"I think this is the highest I've ever been in a building, like, ever," Jughead said, though without the unbridled glee emanating from Archie's every pore.

"I can't believe your friend lives here," I said.

"She's amazing," Veronica said. "She's a lot, though—fair warning."

The elevator doors slid open into an enormous, gleaming open space done up just as stark and modern-clean as the lobby had been. Everything about the space screamed "cool!" and—more quietly, but still with assurance—"expensive!"

It began to hit me in full force just how much of an about-face Veronica's life had taken when she relocated to Riverdale. I don't know if I would have handled it half as well.

"Lexi!" Veronica shouted, running to her friend.

A tall black girl with cheekbones more angled than the lines in the wall hanging strode across the room. "Ronnie! Oh my *god*, the country is agreeing with you, girl!" Her long earrings brushed her shoulders as she moved.

"And these are your friends!" She looked at us, and even though I knew she was probably, on some level, silently judging what she saw, she gave a bright, wide smile so warm I forgot to be annoyed or worried by it. "I've heard all about you," she told us, "and I'm *thrilled* to meet you."

"Dude. This place is *sick*," Archie said. Veronica looked amused. Archie's earnestness was just so . . . *Archie*.

"Well, my parents bought it as a pied-à-terre," she said. "But now my dad has a buyer in China who can pay *way* over market. But I say, first of all: Can he *actually* get his money out? Because *that's* a whole thing now . . ." She rolled her eyes like, "I mean, you know, right?"

And I *didn't* know. Like, on a seismic level, I had no clue. But I wasn't going to admit that. "Oh, yeah, totally," I said, nodding in a way that I hoped looked convincing.

It quickly became clear, I really didn't need to bother. Lexi was more of a blunt, straight-shooter type. As I joined Jug in enjoying the stunning view of Central Park West, she pulled Veronica aside.

"I *wish* you'd told me you had three people coming with you," she hissed.

"What do you mean?" Veronica looked genuinely confused. "I said I was bringing my friends."

"You *said* you were bringing your red-hot model boyfriend," Lexi replied. "Not a Sweet Valley High reject and an extra from *Singles*."

Jughead and I exchanged a look. We probably should've been offended by that, but she kinda nailed it.

Veronica made a face. "What's the problem?"

Lexi folded her arms. "The *issue*," she said, "is that we're meeting the Prep boys at Essex, and I only made the reservation for fourteen. And you *know* what's it's like there Saturdays, it's impossible—"

"Uh, ladies." Juggie stepped forward after a quick nod of reassurance from me. "While Betty and I appreciate your social graces, you don't need to worry about us. I'm more J. D. Salinger than Jay McInerney. We weren't planning on joining the nouveau riche today."

"Jughead's never seen New York before, and I haven't been here since I was a kid," I explained. "We're going to go be tourists!"

Lexi made a face at that, but Veronica looked incredibly relieved, which was one more reason I knew we were doing the right thing.

"You *have* to meet up with us later," Veronica said, and Archie chimed in a semi-desperate, "Yes, please!"

That was the plan, anyway.

∧∧∧

It was a beautiful day, one of the first truly warmer weekends we'd had since winter had turned over to spring, and the sidewalks were crowded with people taking in the butter yellow of the afternoon sunlight and the green budding on trees. From Lexi's apartment, we took the subway to Washington Square, then wandered down Houston Street to the Lower East Side, taking in the endless storefronts: pizza by the slice, rare vinyl, a blinking

neon sign advertising the services of an authentic psychic . . .
This city really did have something for everyone.

"Another one bites the dust," Jughead said, pointing at a darkened storefront across the street. I glanced over.

"LANDMARK SUNSHINE?" I read. "If it's landmarked, how can they tear it down?"

He shook his head. "That's just the name of the management group. Landmark Cinemas. Sunshine was a . . ." He seemed to be struggling for just the right words.

"—a landmark?"

He smirked. "Well, yeah. It was built in 2001. It showed lots of arty movies, not just popcorn stuff." I could hear the scorn in his voice.

"Oh, like that other one closer to NYU—the Angelika." The smell of popcorn wafting outside that one had almost made me dizzy—but we didn't come to New York just to watch a movie. We could do that anywhere.

"Yeah. But, like, shouldn't a city of this size be able to support more than one indie movie theater? It was bad enough when Hiram Lodge bought up the Twilight and demolished it."

Jug shrugged, but I could tell he was more upset than he was letting on. The Twilight had been a metaphorical *and* a literal home for him for years. When it was sold, he felt it. "I can't decide if it's worse for it to be happening in a big city, or a small town," he said.

"It's lousy no matter where it happens," I decided, linking my arm through his. "But—hey!" I was dorking out, I knew it, but I was excited to see something I recognized. And maybe shift the vibe slightly, if possible. "Katz's! That's the deli from *When Harry Met Sally . . .*!"

"'I'll have what she's having,'" Jug quoted, deadpan.

"God, I *love* that movie." I sighed.

Jughead grimaced. "Ugh. It's too convenient and cutesy. You want a great New York movie, give me *Taxi Driver.*"

"But it has such a good message," I insisted, clutching him closer. "I love that they start out as friends."

But Jughead wasn't swayed. "*Do* they, though? Doesn't Billy Crystal want to sleep with Meg Ryan as soon as they meet?"

I didn't know why it was so hard for him to just lean into the romance of the movie. "Well, sure," I protested, "and I think she's attracted to him, too. But they don't go there, do they? They're just friends—for *years*!"

"Okay, no offense, but I think you're missing the whole point of the movie," he huffed.

Well, there's "cynical," and there's "pathologically allergic to cheesy but harmless clichés." "Uh, no," I said slowly, "I'm pretty sure *you* are." Were we . . . starting to sort of have a *fight* about this?

He arched an eyebrow at me. "So you *really* think men and women can just be friends?"

"Sure I do," I said, trying to keep my voice neutral. "Look at me and Archie."

He paused. "No comment."

My stomach twisted. The sky was so blue, and yet the day was beginning to sour. Jug and I had been so in sync when we'd first arrived, but the more we wandered the maze of downtown, the more it seemed like we just weren't on the same page. They say opposites attract, and in some ways, Jug and I were the perfect example of that.

It turned out, maybe not.

I led Jug to the Strand, an indie bookshop just south of Union Square. Its slogan was "eighteen miles of books," and wandering through its cramped, overflowing aisles, I thought that was probably a conservative estimate. Jughead was in heaven. Or, as he put it, "The Noah Baumbach movie version of heaven," which in Jug's world was even better.

"This place is *sublime*," he raved. "I want to move to New York permanently just so I can spend hours here every Saturday."

"I thoroughly support that," I said, "but we've already spent a bunch of time here. Shouldn't we move on? There's so much more to see!"

"But I'm only through the letter *D* in 'True Crime.'"

This wasn't looking promising. I knew he wouldn't be swayed by the mention of going back to Central Park or up to Times Square—he'd already made clear his disdain for those kinds of "tourist traps." I had to get creative.

Aha! I spotted a first edition Julia Child, *My Life in France*, and began paraphrasing a few passages aloud. When I got to the part about roast duck cassoulets, Jughead snapped to attention. "Let's eat."

We found the closest thing to a diner in the immediate vicinity, but it turned out to be utterly hipsterized, which (naturally) made Jughead scoff. There was an ice cream sundae on the menu for one thousand dollars. I pointed out that it had real gold flakes in it, but that didn't impress him. "Is that even safe to eat, gold?"

I tried to laugh him off, but he was on a roll. "And for the record, my hamburger is overcooked, the bun is too bready, and I could buy FOUR of Pop's burgers for the price of this one. Why are we here, again?"

"I don't know," I said, frustrated. "Because it's iconic!" The Fodor's app had recommended it. But that wasn't why I'd suggested this place, really.

"Since when do we care about where people go? Especially when it's a place that has crappy food?"

I swallowed. "My family used to come here, Jug."

He put his burger down and looked at me.

"Every time we came to the city as kids, my parents would take me and Polly here for ice cream sundaes. Not the gold-flaked ones, just vanilla, but still . . ." It made me smile to think of it now. Polly would get chocolate sprinkles and I'd get rainbow, and we'd swap halfway through.

"Everything's been such a mess with Polly since Jason was killed, and you know my mom's hanging on by a thread, pretty much constantly. But I thought, hey, maybe this place hasn't changed. I could have a nice memory. Maybe some ice cream. And you could get your New York burger, too. Bonus." I looked down. "Obviously I made an error in judgment."

Jughead was quiet, taking it all in. "Okay, I'm being a dick," he admitted at last. "I'm sorry." He reached across the booth for my hand. "Where to next? Anywhere you want."

∧∧∧

Bethesda Fountain in Central Park may have been yet another typical "tourist trap," but it didn't disappoint. Jughead and I stood on the steps and watched the water flow from the elegant sculpture, the radiant colors of nature refracting through the reflecting pools. Below us, rowboats slowly crisscrossed the lake. The park smelled lush, green, alive—enough that I felt awake again, almost buoyant. Even after that quasi-disastrous burger break.

"Isn't this beautiful?" I sighed. "This lake is in, like, *every* movie that ever took place in New York."

Jughead shrugged. "Well, every mindless rom-com, yeah."

I bristled. Wasn't he just thirty minutes ago apologizing for shading on my New York City experience? Now he was sulking, again? "So, what? You think your favorite New York movies are better than mine?"

"I didn't say *that*," he protested. "I just mean . . . you like the side of the city that's a little more . . . *glossy*. I prefer the city that's more grimy. More real."

Now it was my turn to shrug. "Sure, Jug."

I knew what he was really saying. I just wasn't ready to hear it.

∧∧∧

From Central Park, it was a short walk to the Dakota building, the imposing but impossibly chic gothic structure whose sharp turrets and gabled rooftop peaks sliced at the sky. It was gorgeous. It was menacing. It fit my mood now.

"Now, *here's* a real piece of New York history," Jughead said. "The Dakota."

"You know Veronica lived here, before her father was arrested, right?" It was hard to imagine, the building was so over-the-top. But then—so was V.

"Yeah. But slightly more culturally significant is that, right there in the doorway? That's where John Lennon was shot. Practically his own doorstep." I couldn't believe it—Jughead actually sounded *swoony* over that gruesome bit of Americana.

"Oh my god," I said. "That's tragic."

"Well, yeah. But still . . . horrible as it was . . . he *did* go out with his legacy intact." Jughead stuffed his hands into his pockets. "Most rock stars of his era who are still alive are either making mediocre music, or they're stuck playing songs they wrote forty years ago. It sucks that he died young, but in a way, it makes our memory of him more . . . *eternal*."

I was silent, thinking.

"What's wrong? Too morbid?" Jughead asked.

I couldn't quite look him in the eye. "We're just . . . *so different*. We don't look at things the same way. We don't like the same things." I paused, tears welling in my eyes. "I don't even know if I really *like* New York." That was it, the living, breathing heart of why this particular sticking point was so . . . sticky.

"What do you mean, you don't like New York?"

"I mean, I *like* it okay, sure. Spending a day here—great." Even though it wasn't really true, this day *hadn't* been all that great. "But, I don't know. Maybe you're right—I think the things I like about it, the places I know—maybe they aren't the real city." *Maybe our differences were just too much. Or would be, eventually.*

Jughead was my high school sweetheart, after all. And who even ends up with their high school sweetheart in the long run, anyway? My mom and dad got married out of high school—not exactly a ringing endorsement of that life choice.

Jughead looked truly alarmed. "Betty, I was just being mean," he said. "I said I'd stop, I should have tried harder. I don't know what's wrong with me. I don't—"

"Do you think you'll ever live here?" I cut him off.

He stiffened. "Well, *someday*, yeah. I always dreamed I'd live on the Lower East Side, or in Brooklyn. Spend my twenties here before moving to a small town in Maine, like Stephen King." His eyes were sad, pensive. "Don't you think you'll live here, too?"

Moment of truth, Betty. It was the question I didn't want to answer. But here it was.

"Honestly? Not really, no."

Now I *did* look at him. "I keep thinking back to my internship in LA last summer. I *loved* it there. I've been thinking about maybe . . . going to college out there." This felt like one of the most terrifying confessions I could possibly make to Jughead, especially here and now. I took a deep breath and blurted out the rest of it.

"Jughead, what's going to happen to us? You know . . . after high school?"

There it was. A simple question with no pat, easy response.

And so he just stood there, stammering, because: There was nothing he *could* say, no thread he could possibly pull that wouldn't completely unravel the illusion we had created. The elaborate fiction that the world beyond Riverdale would never intrude or impose on our lives.

In the end, he didn't have to answer. He was saved by the bell.

Really, the car horn. It was Veronica and Archie. At first I was confused, wondering how they'd known where to find us, but it turned out they'd wanted to drive past the Dakota so Veronica could have a look at her older, grander stomping grounds.

"And honestly, I'm kind of regretting it," she joked, leaning out of the open car window to call to us. "Because the Dakota makes the Pembrooke look like something out of that *Worst Room* blog." She rolled her eyes.

We all decided we were ready to head back to Riverdale. Veronica and Archie were cozy on the car ride back, in their own world, holding hands and whispering inside jokes back and forth.

"You know, I kind of love New York," Archie said.

"There's nowhere like it," Veronica agreed. "But for now, I'm glad to be going home."

"You *cannot* have had as good a day as us," Archie said.

He didn't mean it like a challenge, or even to gloat. I know Archie; he was just excited, and in love. It made me think:

For Archie and Veronica, their differences brought them closer together. But for Jughead and me, they had unearthed questions that neither of us were ready to answer.

"You know what?" I sounded bitter, but I couldn't help myself. "I'm sure you're right, Archie."

Jughead and I were silent as the car drove up the West Side Highway, the river looking black and bottomless in the moonlight.

The world beyond Riverdale called us. We all knew that. Someday, when we were old enough, it would threaten our relationships, our friendships . . . even our town itself. We knew now, all of us, that the day would come.

But in that moment, despite the abysmal fail our impromptu day trip had been? I still thought we had more time.

I had no idea, then, just exactly how much I didn't know.

$$\sim\sim\sim$$

Back in the moment, in the cold, dark quiet of Veronica's lake house, I clutched Jughead, caught up in the melancholy memory. "That day. There were some fun memories." I tried, as always, to focus on those.

"Yep." Jughead was eager to agree. Eager to pretend, too, every now and then. But then his tone shifted, and he got more real. "But it definitely left us feeling shaky about—I don't know, real life. The future. Where we'd end up."

"I was so worried, that whole drive back," I said. It felt good to be so straightforward with him. "All I could see was our sell-by date, looming. And then we got back, and we fell back into a rhythm, and things were good—"

"Things were <u>great</u>," he said, kissing me.

"Yes, <u>great</u>. Epic. And now..."

Now it's all unraveling, anyway, I thought. I couldn't bring myself to say it aloud. Now I wonder if we were just in denial, all along.

Jughead brushed my cheek with his finger. "I know."

I was glad not to have to explain myself. Jug and I were stronger than ever, that was for sure. But it wasn't enough. It wasn't enough to keep our world from spinning out.

There was a sudden, sharp suction sound, like an airtight seal being broken, and the house groaned to life around us. I blinked at the lights, which felt searing after the blackout.

"Power's up," Jughead said. "Should we go check on the others?"

I nodded, but we were still pulling ourselves up to stand when they flung open the door to the cellar. Veronica looked flushed but triumphant. "Never underestimate a Hiram Lodge fail-safe," she said. "We're fine. That's over. What a relief."

It <u>was</u> a relief. For the moment.

But it wasn't really true.

Nothing was over.

And I feared nothing would ever be truly "fine" again.

~~~

Back upstairs, it was Archie who raised some still-outstanding bad news.

"I hate to say it, guys, but those—uh, those birds are still out there." He looked truly repulsed, thinking about them again. "Jug and I can clean them up. We'll be quick."

"And if this were medieval Europe, Betty and I might allow that impressive display of misogyny disguised as chivalry, Archiekins," Veronica said. "But seeing as it's the twenty-first century, and—surprise!—just like Ginger Rogers, the so-called fairer sex can do anything you boys can do, but backwards and in heels—we'll pitch in." She shot me a quick look and I nodded my agreement. "Eight hands are faster than four. And we have miles to go before we sleep."

I could see it on Archie's face: that complicated mix of love, pride, and sorrow. He didn't want Veronica to have to clean up his mess. But he was misunderstanding something vital:

It was _our_ mess. Not just his. That was the part he still wasn't getting.

I began to roll up my sleeves, literally. "Come on, Archie. We've got this."

"One small step for B and V, one giant leap for feminism," Veronica said. She didn't look thrilled at the prospect of the chore that was ahead of us. But she _did_ look determined. "If nothing else, this will be an excellent reason to upgrade these shoes with those embellished Jimmy Choo booties I've been eyeing at Stacks Fifth Avenue."

"There's that bright side we were all hoping for," Jughead said.

We all managed a small laugh at that. But just barely.

∧∧∧

It was messy work, but V was right—with all four of us focused, it was over quickly. (Not that that fact made it any less gross.) Before _too_ long, we were all sweaty and huffing, an uncharacteristically disheveled Veronica triumphantly hoisting a huge black trash bag over one shoulder. A stray curl swayed against her forehead and she shook her head, sending it off her face and out of her eyes.

"You know," she mused, "when I was at the Ashram's Mallorca outpost last New Year's with Bella Hadid, a swami there told me that crows are bad luck. And I have to say, I've never believed that more."

"I'm not gonna ask what 'the Ashram' is," Jughead said, "but it's pretty hard to argue that a pile of dead birds would ever be <u>good</u> luck. It's called a 'murder' of crows, you know. Inauspicious."

"You made that up," Archie said.

"Trust me, Arch, I am not that creative."

For the umpteenth time since his arrest, I saw a wave of panic flash across Archie's face. "Come on, you guys," I said, "this is Archie's life. We're not gonna get distracted by dumb superstitions."

"Betty's right," Veronica chimed in. "Not even a Goop-endorsed swami's suggestions are sacrosanct." She passed the trash bag off to Archie, who began walking it down the long drive to where the animal-proof bins were stored. "So what now?"

"I don't know about you guys, but I'm starving," Jughead said.

We both stared at him. "What?" he asked, smiling.

"Let me see if I've got this straight," Veronica said. "A murdered murder of crows is just what it takes to ignite your appetite?"

"Haven't you learned yet, Veronica? My appetite doesn't need igniting. It's ever-present. Like—sadly—the ubiquitousness of Goop."

"Fair enough," she said. "Though I can't say it was on the top of my to-do list, we could probably all use a refuel. Are we all good with the same bedrooms as last time?" Everyone nodded. "Then let's drop the luggage, wash up, and have a midnight snack."

Jughead gave me first dibs on the shower—chivalrous, yes, sexist, maybe—but I definitely wasn't going to argue with him with the possible remnants of Shadow Lake bird flu slime still slick on my hands. I turned the water to scalding, let the room fill with steam, and dove into what can best be described as an extreme <u>Silkwood</u> shower.

I was toweling off when I realized my hands were shaking again. My eyes were hot and bleary, too, through the fog of the bathroom mirror. This night was endless. And Veronica was right: miles to go, yet.

I glanced at my jeans, bundled in a heap on the bathroom floor. The Adderall bottle was tucked in a back pocket; I'd snatched it from my purse before the shower just in case. Meanwhile, it was the dead of night, the power had already gone out once, and my skin was on fire. Did I need another fix?

I was holding my jeans in one hand, the Adderall bottle in the other, considering the worse-and-worser options when I heard it. A little blip, a chirp, an overture.

My cell phone. I'd brought that into the bathroom, too.

It was ringing. Aggressively. Insistently. The ringing went on and on.

And not just any ringing, either.

My phone was playing "Lollipop." A seemingly innocuous oldie pop song that left my blood cold.

"Lollipop"—otherwise known as the Black Hood's ringtone.

This isn't real, I thought, desperate. It can't be. We caught you. You were my father, and we got you, and you're locked up.

But if it wasn't real, then why wouldn't the phone <u>stop ringing</u>?

I pressed the "ignore" button, trying to shut it off. UNKNOWN ID, the screen blinked, taunting me. Frustrated, I threw the phone on the vanity, hearing it clatter on impact.

"Betty, you okay in there?" Jughead sounded easy enough. So he'd heard something—something that made him want to check on me. But nothing truly concerning. Not the exact ringtone. Of that, I was sure. He would've broken the door down at the first note.

"I'm fine!" I called, breathing deep and trying to will it true. I glanced at the pill bottle in my hand. The cap was off now.

<u>What?</u> When had that happened?

The faucet was running, too.

Had I taken a pill? More than one? How could I not remember?

Growing frantic, I screwed the cap back on the pills—I'd count them later, when my head was clearer—jumped back into my clothes, and put the bottle in my pocket again. Every particle of my body stood at attention—and I couldn't be sure why. The phantom phone call? A chemical reaction? All or none of the above?

"Can I get in there? Not to rush you, but I'm dying to rinse off the Ebola virus. I'm worried if I marinate too long, I'll go mutant zombie on you guys."

"Of course! One second!" I grabbed my phone and flipped it over. Maybe there was some way of tracing the anonymous call—if not now, then later, when we were home again and this was all a hilarious, distant nightmare of a memory.

The screen <u>had</u> cracked when I tossed the phone. A hairline sliver, snaking across the glass like a fork of lightning. With a cold fist of dread clenched in my stomach, I scrolled to the call log.

NO MISSED CALLS.

I shook my head and looked again.

NO MISSED CALLS.

I forced my voice to sound normal. "I'm coming," I told Jug.

It was that or start going truly insane.

CHAPTER SIXTEEN

JUGHEAD

One of the other unexpected benefits of having access to a Hiram Lodge second home was a seemingly endless flow of hot water, something my family had never known in the trailer park. Say what you will about the megalomaniacal tycoon— and I've said plenty, and could (and probably would) say plenty more—the man knew how to outfit a cabin in the woods.

Betty took her time in the shower, while I lay on the bed watching steam curl under the door, considering our night so far, the evidence we had (not much), and what we were still looking for (anything that would implicate Hiram and therefore exonerate one Archie Andrews).

To say that it all felt like the longest of long shots was . . .

Nope. I forced myself to push that thought away. Betty wouldn't have any of that, I knew. She had plenty of her own inner demons, I'd seen them time and again, did my best to help her hold them at bay, but when it came to her friends, she was relentlessly hopeful. I could stand to take a page—or a chapter, even—from her book.

So then this was it, our own personal bizarro-world version of that old-school game show where you had to guess your partner's answers in order to win: *What Would Betty Do?* If she were trying to sway me away from these negative thoughts, what would she tell me?

That was easy. She'd suggest—no, *insist*—I investigate all angles. We'd done it together, often enough.

All angles . . . like maybe those housed in Hiram Lodge's innermost sanctum?

Which would have to be his study. He had one at the Pembrooke, he must have had one at the Dakota, and I was sure he had one here. At least one. If ever there were a man who needed an entire collection of closets to stash away his army of skeletons, it was Veronica's father.

Okay, so I had to find them and search them. Thoroughly.

I knocked on the bathroom door. There was a small beat, and then it opened a crack. Betty peered out, wrapped in a towel and looking slightly wild-eyed.

"Everything okay?" She didn't look as relaxed as I would have expected, coming out of a steamy shower. Of course, this wasn't exactly a relaxing jaunt to the lake house.

"Of course," she said quickly, in a not-altogether-convincing tone. "Sorry, I've been awhile."

"No, it's no problem," I assured her. "That's actually why I was knocking. To let you know to relax for a minute. There are at least three other bathrooms in this place. I'll use the one in the guest room next door. Meet you in the kitchen?"

"Oh! Sure." Her eyes darted past me, over my shoulder, and then came back to meet my gaze. "Good idea."

"You sure you're all right?"

"Why wouldn't I be?" She gave me a quick kiss, enveloping me in the heavy floral scent of whatever shampoo she'd just used.

"Other than the fact that we're here revisiting the site of a violent home invasion in the hopes of rescuing our falsely accused friend from possible jail time? Oh—and let's not forget the Welcome Wagon pile of bloody birds. Some people might find all that a little bit stressful. Just, you know, for starters."

"I'm *fine*," she insisted, sounding more like herself now. "*Some* people aren't from Riverdale, remember?" She passed a dry towel to me and pushed me away from the open door. "We have experience with these sort of things there."

I stared at the closed door, amused and a little bewildered. Betty had that effect on me. "How could I possibly forget?"

∧∧∧

After a quick shower, I found Hiram's office down the hall on the second floor. The door was ajar or I would never have noticed it, which might have been the first little bit of luck I'd stumbled onto all night. I hoped it wouldn't be my last.

The room was decorated straight out of *Alpha Male Mobster's Digest*, which I guessed was probably his overall aesthetic for all his personal man-cave needs. Dark leather, paneled walls, some kind of dead animal skin on the floor, an enormous fireplace, and various taxidermy busts on the wall. In the corner was a bar cart that looked to be antique, crowded with bottles and stocked with cut-crystal tumblers. It was all very *Goodfellas* by way of *The Shining*.

I wanted to be discreet; even if Veronica was fully on board with her father as the Big Bad in our current horror show, there was something awkward about rifling through his personal space behind her back. Assuming I found something during my snooping, I could better justify my choice in doing so.

So, you're just gonna have to find something, Jones, I thought, scanning the office. A file cabinet stood in the far corner, the same burnished wood as the gleaming desk and side tables spaced throughout. But when I tried the handles, they were locked. I don't know why I was surprised at that. The top drawer of his desk was locked, too. Obviously.

The situation called for Betty. We were better together, in general. She was also the true Nancy Drew of our duo. I was more like an only-*slightly*-more-useful Ned Nickerson, if we're being honest.

My gaze caught on a bookshelf against the back wall. Specifically, the ancient Underwood resting on it, its keys looking like nothing more than row after row of teeth, black and strong. Betty had gotten me an antique typewriter like this one last Christmas. Funny how that gift had seemed thoughtful and unique, whereas this one here seemed filled with menace.

It's all about the context, I thought, remembering even more of my Stephen King. Paul Sheldon had killed Annie Wilkes with a similar machine in the original novel of *Misery*. Menacing, indeed. *We're your number one fans, Hiram.*

It was hard to believe it was Veronica's *father* out to ruin Archie's life. But it would have been harder to believe had Jason Blossom not been killed by his own father just a year before. Betty was right—we Riverdale kids had a different sort of conditioning. Our rites of passage were decidedly grimmer. But I guess they toughened us up, too.

When they didn't outright kill us.

"What are you doing in here?"

Crap. Busted. I looked up to see an uncharacteristically dressed-down Veronica peering at me through her oversized reading glasses from the doorway of the room.

Just combing through your father's personal files without telling you. But I hadn't found anything—yet—and thus couldn't bring myself to cop to that truth. "I, uh—I was looking for a shower, so Betty could have more time in ours. Saw the door open here and caught a glimpse of that Underwood. It's a beauty."

"It is. No doubt some gift from another loyal crime syndicate subject, an attempt at bribing Daddykins to keep him placated." She rolled her eyes. "As if he types his own memos. He's far too Don Draper for such trivialities."

I shrugged. "It could be just for show. An objet, isn't that what they're called? Or maybe he uses it for some of his . . . sensitive documents, you know? Stuff you wouldn't want saved on a hard drive." Suddenly, a lightbulb flickered in my brain. *What if* . . .

But before I could think on it further, Veronica raised an eyebrow. "You wouldn't happen to be in here in the hopes of accidentally landing on some of those sensitive documents yourself?"

"Uh . . ." I smiled sheepishly.

"Not to worry, Jughead, I get it—that's why we're here, after all. We can come back up and give everything a thorough search after we eat."

"Good plan." And a relief to know she truly was all in on proving Archie's innocence—even at the expense of her father's guilt.

"In the meantime, though, you're free to pore over every corner of this place with a fine-tooth comb. By all means, leave no stone unturned. But let's not go out of our way to leave a trace."

"Of course not." That didn't even need to be said (though Veronica obviously disagreed).

"That includes not straight-up *announcing* our presence, Jug," she said, sighing like she was a patient teacher addressing a particularly wild kindergartener.

"Of course *not*." I looked at her. "Wait—what do you mean? You seem like you're referring to something specific."

She walked toward me, brisk. Her cashmere lounge set made a *swish*ing sound, like a whisper, as she strode. "Jug." She tapped her finger on the window. "Just a touch OTT, don't you think?"

Over the top. But what was she pointing at? I looked.

It was a crown, my traditional tag, drawn in ragged, hasty freehand—an index finger against the condensation of the window. I stared at it. "How . . . *The Lady Vanishes*."

"Exactly." Veronica wrapped her fist in her sweater and rubbed at it until the image was an unrecognizable smear. "In other words, by definition, too much. So just, be more careful. No harm done. I'm going to run down to the wine cellar to get us a bottle of something full-bodied to sip with our post-midnight snack. Nothing to muddy our minds, but I think we could all stand to take the slightest of edges off."

"I . . . don't disagree." I blinked at the smear and the crown sketch was back, wavery but distinct.

Another blink, and it was gone again.

Was I already too muddy?

If I did take the edge off, what would I see then? Would the crown come back, again?

I wasn't so sure I wanted to find out.

"Just keep it ten percent more on the DL, Encyclopedia Brown," Veronica said. "Meet us downstairs in five."

"Of course. Sure. Yeah." I didn't turn from the window, just listened to her *swish* out of the room and pad down the hall.

Ten percent more on the DL. I could do that. I knew I could.

I didn't know if I could promise no more crowns, though, for one simple reason:

I hadn't been the one to draw that crown in the first place.

∧∧∧

JOSIE

Our first stop after Reggie's party? Venom's lair. We had spray cans, and the Pussycats weren't above a little light artistic expression in the name of intimidating our competition.

"Girl, you know how to show them what we've got," Val said, surveying my handiwork.

Nine lives are better than one, the graffiti read. Call it our motto.

"I'm only sorry the paint is temporary," I said. "We'll have to challenge them to an encore when the rain washes this gorgeous tribute away."

"You know it," Melody said.

Maybe she meant it, maybe she didn't. But it was nice to hear.

"Your turn," I said to her. "Where to next?"

"The community pool." She grinned. "Swimming's always better after hours."

"I like the way you think," I approved. "Val?"

"Pop's," she said. "I like to stick with the classics. A little milk shake, a little dancing . . . on the booth tables."

"Think bigger," I suggested. "Dancing on tables is a classic, sure, but we know counters are great, too. Sort of *Coyote Ugly* with less white girl nonsense and not even ironically ugly."

Her eyes lit up. "Excellent."

My phone, tucked into my back pocket, buzzed. Sweet Pea, probably. Or Reggie.

Either way, I just ignored it. I didn't have time for that noise right now.

∧∧∧

Cheryl:

Josephine, am I to understand from TeeTee that you've been spending some time with Sweet Pea while we've been away? How did I not realize?

Cheryl:

May I just say: Get it, girl! (I respect your right to privacy—but only to an extent, of course, as I do have an obligation to keep one eye on my Vixens and their so-called extracurriculars at all times.)

Cheryl:

In any case, Toni apparently had a few semi-cryptic exchanges with him earlier this evening, and is simply apoplectic that he's now gone incommunicado.

Cheryl:

On the chance that you do happen to hear from him tonight, would you mind being a dear and mentioning that my Serpent paramour is trying to reach your Serpent paramour?

Cheryl:

Tx & toodles!

∿∿∿

Dilton:

Haven't heard from your contact yet.

Sweet Pea:

You will. Sit tight. And while you're at it, lose my number.

‿‿‿

PP:

Got your name from our mutual friend. Do you have what I need? Can you do the job?

Dilton:

For a fee, sure.

PP:

I'm sure we can work something out. My boys will be in touch.

CHAPTER SEVENTEEN

VERONICA

It was almost funny how obviously guilty Jughead looked pillaging my father's study behind my back, given that the whole point of this trip to the lake was to pillage for evidence. *Almost* funny . . . until I stopped and reflected on how adamant Betty and Jughead had been the last time we were up here that my father was beyond redemption, and that whatever machinations he'd put into play were going to undo not only the four of us but everything we loved and held dear back in Riverdale. I hadn't wanted to hear it then, hadn't been ready . . . but once Daddy decided that Archie's very existence was merely collateral damage amidst our ongoing personal War of the Roses . . .

Well, that was the exact moment when it ceased being "funny," to the extent that it ever had been in the first place.

And credit where credit is due, props to Jug and Betty for never saying "I told you so."

Suffice it to say, if I'd found Jughead rummaging around in my father's files the last time we were here, it could have been the final nail in the coffin of our four-way friendship.

Things were tense enough between us, that trip. Today, though, our little band of would-be Robin Hood–esque marauders represented our own last hope for justice.

As it was, I was more than happy to give Jughead a little more time in that office. As long as he didn't go leaving a proverbial calling card in every corner of this house.

Then again, the thought of ruining Daddy's plot *and* rubbing his nose in it?

Well, I can't say it wasn't tempting.

∧∧∧

The Lodge Lodge wine cellar is older than the lodge itself. It was here, once upon a time, when this building was still an inn, and not a one-family vacation home. Daddy renovated this place himself (or rather, he paid dozens of architects and contractors to renovate it *for* him), with a lot of guidance and aesthetic vision from my mother. But as he likes to boast to our weekend guests, the cellar didn't need to be touched. It was commercial-grade, of course, because at one point it had *been* a commercial cellar, and it was commercial-*sized* as well. It was temperature-regulated at an ideal fifty-five degrees, which felt chilly after that warm shower. The space was designed to look like a Tuscan wine cave, with wide stone tiling and endless rows of wine racks neatly stacked in per-fect wooden squares.

I went straight to the most valuable bottles in the collection. They were easy to pinpoint, even if you hadn't grown up around such luxuries. They were notable for how my father stored them: sideways, labels out, the better to impress any company who might be on a casual tour. Some of these bottles were worth more than my mother's engagement ring. I didn't have to be a professional sommelier to know that.

Scanning all those pretty labels, embossed with gold leaf and soft as silk, I had a moment of semi-weakness. Or, maybe the better way to think about it was that I chose to pace myself when it came to exacting revenge. I decided to pull my punches ever so slightly.

I snatched up a Domaine Leroy Musigny Grand Cru, a pinot noir that my mother loved to enjoy by the fire on a crisp autumn evening, and that my father acquired at auction for $8,400. (This was considered a steal.) The $350,000 champagne I decided we'd come back for, to toast Archie's freedom after this whole sordid mess was behind us.

See? Pacing myself. I didn't have to choose one over the other when there would be time enough for both.

The pilfered pinot would hurt enough, for now, once he realized it had been stolen out from under him and enjoyed by the very young man whose life he was dead set on ruining.

Once I had it in my hand, fingers wrapped around the delicate embossing of the label, I crept down the hallway to take a reassuring peek at the generator. It was a standby model, which was also commercial-grade, and completely fail-safe in the event of just about anything short of a full-blown apocalypse. Daddy kept it in the security center, also in the basement, a veritable surveillance bank of closed-circuit camera screens, backup equipment like the genny, and other in-case-of-emergency-break-glass types of products, like high-end lanterns and first-aid supplies. The security room was accessed through a panel in Daddy's downstairs office—it was, as the others had pointed out, extremely archvillain-esque. I meant to check it before, when Archie and I disabled the alarm, but then the power went out, and by the time it came back on, Betty and Jughead were on the other side of the door and there was crows' blood to be mopped.

Just another Saturday night in Veronica Lodge's current waking nightmare.

Now I punched the code into the panel's keypad—the same combination as the alarm: my birthday, always my birthday—and ducked into the long, skinny space through a slanted door. To a casual observer, it would have looked like nothing more than a closet or storage space.

I had talked with my friends about disabling the cameras, and we'd decided against that. Too risky, given that we weren't sure who or what might be tracking us. I glanced around the room. The generator stood in one corner, bulky and imposing, blinking green, which meant it was charged and ready to go. But not *on* right now, so whatever had caused the brief blackout, it had passed and the grid was back up and running. I tried to decide if that information was in any way useful, but for now it was mainly just comforting. We had power.

. . . Or *did* we? Looking closer at the row of security monitors—sixteen in all, stacked like a checkerboard—one was blaring nothing but fuzz. Static.

The camera was out. But we *hadn't* disabled any. We had talked about it. And then I'd been briefly distracted.

I peered at the neat little screens. One showed the entrance to the drive. There was one trained on each bedroom and the study—there was Jughead, still staring, more than a little confused, out the window where I'd seen his crown tag.

There were a few positioned through different checkpoints in the woods and one at the back door of the house. One hovered over the hot tub like a lecherous old man, leering.

Footage, I realized. Footage from that night would be extremely useful. Footage from the woods, where Andre and Archie encountered Cassidy in the first place.

A cursory sweep of the back tapes made it clear, though, that if the footage existed at all—and knowing Daddy, I'm certain it did—it wasn't here. At least, it was nowhere obvious to be found.

And the camera that was out?

That was the camera positioned at the front door . . . the camera that would have told us who, exactly, had left those birds for us.

How long had this camera been down? I could have kicked myself for not checking the cameras when Archie and I first came down here, like I'd said I would. Then I might have had a better idea if it was just a glitch, or a result of the power outage . . .

Or if someone else had deactivated that camera deliberately.

The same someone who'd dropped those birds on my doorstep, for example.

It was easy enough to understand why such a person might want that footage destroyed.

The hard part would be proving any of this.

Assuming, of course, that if someone *was* keeping tabs on us? Deliberately terrorizing us?

Assuming we made it out of here at all.

CHAPTER EIGHTEEN

ARCHIE

"I'm just going to run down to the wine cellar. I'll pick us out something dry and cozy to sip on while we put together our investigative game plan," Veronica said.

She was standing in the doorway of our bedroom, the same one we'd shared last time—the same one from where she'd pressed the panic button that had alerted Andre to the intruders, but I pushed those thoughts (*dark eyes dark hoods baseball bats*) out of my head as quickly as I could.

I blinked—*green eyes black hood*—and when I opened my eyes, I was safe. There was Veronica again, wearing some kind of soft purple sweater-y drawstring pants with a matching robe and silky top underneath. Even her casual clothes were fancy. She was wearing those cute oversized reading glasses she usually saves for hanging out at home, and her eyes were dark and intent, peering at me through the lenses. Her hair was still damp, leaving wet patches at either shoulder of her robe.

"You're okay, right?" She looked very worried.

"Of course!" I was trying to sound definite, but it was a little too much, too loud for the two of us standing so close together. I lowered my voice and stepped closer to her. "I'm fine," I said again. I don't know how well she believed me, but she left it alone. She stood on her tiptoes and gave me a kiss.

"So you'll meet us downstairs to eat something in a few minutes?"

I nodded. "Yeah. I just want to put some stuff away."

She headed down to the cellar, and I went to put my toothbrush and other toiletries into the bathroom. There wasn't much to unpack, really, since we'd all just grabbed what we'd need for the one night.

We didn't *have* more than one night to work this out, anyway. It was literally now or never. To sort out my own maybe-forever.

Coming back out of the bathroom, I grabbed the sweater I'd thrown on the bed. I'd just tossed it there before I got into the shower, so now I shrugged it back on. It was only once I was dressed that I realized the pillows on my side of the bed were kind of out of place. Not in any major way, not so you'd notice if you weren't like I was, sort of staring off into space at the bed, in a zone. But given that everything in all the Lodges' homes was always perfect, arranged just so, it made me stop.

A chill came over me then. It was like something out of a movie, like this sudden sense that I was being watched, or that something important, something that would mean a lot, in the end, was about to happen. I once saw a documentary about a person who had dissociative states, and I felt the way he'd described it in the movie—like I wasn't here, all of a sudden, just disconnected from my body and floating way above the scene, watching it from somewhere far away.

I forced myself to clench my hand, remembering that I could do that, I was a person with a body, and I reached for the pillow.

It was warm.

That doesn't mean anything, I told myself. *What if Veronica had sat there, or lay down there, just for a minute? It would be warm then, wouldn't it? That wouldn't be weird.*

I picked it up, but the pillow didn't smell like the stuff Veronica uses in her hair, or that lotion that makes me think of vanilla ice cream. It just smelled like clean laundry.

Then I looked back down at the bed.

It took a second for me to realize what I was looking at.

It was a note.

On the bed, underneath where the pillow had been, was a note. A piece of paper, just plain white and jagged around the edges, like it'd been ripped from a larger piece of paper. The writing was in blocky black print.

The message made my stomach churn.

I KNOW WHAT YOU DID.

That was it. That was all it said, in bold, heavy scrawl. There was no signature, not even an initial. Not that I was expecting one.

Every muscle in my body tensed. My first instinct was to run to the windows, to check that we were safe (*safe*—like that was a word that even had any meaning in our world anymore). I rushed over and looked, shoving the curtains aside.

Nothing. There was nothing out there but the sound of the wind and the crickets. But then, those were the same things we'd heard, that night.

The first night here. The night that started everything. The night we were attacked.

It had been completely and utterly quiet that night, too. Until the minute that it hadn't been. The second that we heard a crash, and our hackles went up, and all of a sudden, everything changed.

Who wrote this? Did Hiram leave it for us to find? No, that didn't make sense; our parents didn't know we were even here. Had someone followed us inside the lodge? Maybe whoever left those birds?

It was like something out of Jughead's horror movies: *I know what you did*. But it was happening to us, in real life.

Shame washed over me. My friends, they wouldn't even be here if it weren't for me. Had I led them straight back into danger by agreeing to come here?

I folded and unfolded the note in my hand. It wasn't a hallucination, as much as I wanted it to be.

I know what you did.

But I *hadn't* killed Cassidy; that wasn't me. I'd chased him into the woods, sure. And when I saw Andre there, standing over him, I'd looked Andre straight in the eye. I didn't know, exactly, what he was going to do, but I couldn't claim *complete* innocence, either. On some level, I knew, had at least a small sense of what would come next. But I didn't say anything or intervene, or even stay to bear witness. I'd looked at Andre, and then I'd turned and walked away.

And *then* I'd heard gunshots.

I'd done a lot of things since I'd met Hiram Lodge. I'd started the Red Circle. I'd claimed to have killed Papa Poutine on behalf of Mr. Lodge. I'd threatened Sweet Pea with a gun, even though I (probably) would never have used it. All real, true facts that my mom had warned me would probably come up in the prosecution's closing arguments.

I know what you did.

The thing about that note was, it could have been talking about so many things.

I may not have killed Cassidy, but I'd done plenty.

And someone out there knew it.

Someone out there was watching. And they understood that even if I wasn't guilty, I wasn't exactly innocent, either.

When I got downstairs, Betty, Jughead, and Veronica were seated at one end of the massive dining table. There was a platter with bread and cold cuts laid out, and Jug was piling about six sandwiches' worth of turkey onto a slice of white.

"Archie!" Veronica's eyes lit up. She held out a glass of wine to me and, when I took it, tapped her own against it gently in a cheers.

"Hey, guys." The note from the bedroom was burning a hole in my pocket, but I didn't say anything about it. I wasn't ready to just yet.

"Have a seat." Veronica gestured at the spread. In addition to sandwich fixings, there was a huge bowl of cut fruit and another, even bigger, bowl of chips. Several cans of soda were popped open in addition to the four wine glasses that had already been poured, and some plastic water bottles and a half-empty carafe of coffee. And next to Jughead's plate was a bag of peanut M&M's almost bigger than he was.

"Chocolate and cola," he said, noticing me noticing. "With a chaser of black coffee. A little sugar-and-caffeine boost to get us through the witching hour."

"There's nothing *little* about that, Juggie," Betty joked.

But she was drinking from her own soda a lot more eagerly than her wine, I saw.

"Help yourself, Archie," Veronica said. "We'll fortify and recap all our current intel. Then we can strategize. We have turkey, ham, chicken, pretty much every cheese available for purchase pre-sliced, and good old-fashioned PB&J."

"Also these amazing oatmeal cookies that were in the pantry. From some fancy New York bakery." Betty held up a cellophane sleeve closed with a sticker whose logo I dimly recognized.

I hadn't thought I was hungry, but eyeing the table, my stomach growled. I piled a plate high—topping it off with plenty of chips and chocolate, Jug was definitely onto something—and sat down to dig in.

"So," Veronica said, adjusting her glasses at the bridge of her nose. "To recap. What information do we have?"

Tell them, I thought, actually having to hold myself back from taking out the note. I would, I had to . . . but I wasn't ready to yet. Because: *Was* it even information, really? A note that could have come from anyone? At any time? How was that helpful? How was that anything other than more stress?

Hiding things wasn't the answer, either, I knew. But I guess I just . . . needed more time.

"Uh, not much, except for the dead crows," Jughead said. "Also those twins being creepy, back at the General Store."

He took a swig of his soda. "In other words, standard slasher movie fare."

"Not helpful," Betty said.

"I beg to differ," Jughead said. "Extremely helpful. If we're characters in a horror movie, at least there are guidelines and tropes we can refer to."

Veronica raised an eyebrow. "Such as?"

"Have none of you seen *Scream*?" Jughead looked very disappointed in us.

Betty raised her hand smugly. Jughead looked at her. "I know *you* have, Betty, since we watched it together last Halloween. So you're familiar with the rules. Therefore, you have the best chance of survival."

"Enlighten the rest of us, Jughead," Veronica said.

"Okay, so here's how it goes, in that movie. If you want to survive a horror movie, number one: Never have sex. It's a classic virgin/slut dichotomy. If you have sex in a horror movie, you will die shortly thereafter."

"How . . . quaintly puritanical." Veronica actually looked a little amused.

"Don't drink or do drugs," Jug said, counting off the rules on his fingers.

"I guess we all failed that one. Is it too late to switch over to water?" I said, staring at the wine glass in my hand. I meant it like a joke, but it sounded hollow.

"It is *definitely* too late, Archie," Jughead confirmed. "Last but not least, if you want to survive the movie, you can never, ever say 'I'll be right back.' It's like a magic incantation, those words. Kiss of death right there. Say it, and you're guaranteeing you absolutely will not be back. No matter what."

"Ooh," Veronica said, laughing a little herself now. "I guess I violated the handbook myself. When I went down to the wine cellar I specifically told Archie to meet at the dining table, and that I'd be right back."

She was joking, of course, but what she was saying made the hairs on the back of my neck stand up. *Your friends are in danger, Archie. And all because of you.* Maybe not necessarily horror movie danger, like Jughead was detailing. But the consequences were basically the same.

I wanted to speak up, finally, and tell them about the note. Instead, what I did was snap at Jughead. "This is real life, Jug. Not a horror movie. Come on. Let's get back to reality." *I know what you did.* It was real life, *and* it was a horror movie. And I couldn't bring myself to tell the truth.

If Jughead noticed the edge in my voice, though, he didn't let on. He stayed casual, in spite of the subject matter. "Are you serious. Arch? You honestly haven't noticed that our lives basically *are* a horror movie? Jason Blossom, the Black Hood . . . We are, like, one zombie apocalypse away from going full-on *Evil Dead*."

"Okay, well, aside from the fact that you obviously forgot to put away your Halloween decorations last year, Jug, how, exactly, would we fare if this were a *Scream*-style cinematic meta-treatment of our lives?" Veronica took a sip of her wine, totally unbothered by this conversation. That made one of us.

"You really wanna know?"

Veronica nodded, and Jughead laid it out. "Well, I hate to tell you guys, but you two"—he waved a butter knife at Ronnie, then me—"would be the first to be dispatched. Popular hot bitch and her horny, jock boyfriend? Everyone wants to see them go first."

Veronica made a face at my stereotypes, and Betty quickly interjected. "Not us, though," she said.

"No, not *us*," Jug agreed. "We don't want you taken out. But we have no say if we're in the movie with you. We're targets just like you. Besides, I'd be next, anyway. Sardonic, sarcastic, quippy loner sidekick? Yeah, I've got a target on my back."

"So we'd all be doomed," Veronica said.

"All except Betty," Jug corrected her. "She's our Final Girl. The Sidney, the Nancy, the Laurie Strode. She's even blond, which is common. Most recently reimagined in the form of Buffy the Vampire Slayer, the ultimate Final Girl. She actually has mystical powers to help her kick boogey-man ass."

"If only," Betty mused. She had her hand in her pocket and looked like she was fidgeting with something in there—her phone? Maybe.

"Oh, no doubt," Jug said. "I'd probably be killed trying to save you. Valiant but doomed. That would enrage you and put you in exactly the right headspace to kill the monster once and for all. You'd be put through the wringer, but emerge triumphant. And you might even do it in your nightgown, à la Ripley."

"Triumphant. I like that. Except the monster always comes back," she mused, her eyes going vacant for a second.

Everyone went quiet for a beat. Jughead's little jokey diatribe had hit us all a little too close to home. I stood by my first comment. We didn't need to compare our situation to a horror movie, because our actual situation was horrific enough. More than any of the others knew, thanks to my cowardice.

No one wanted to be the one to say it, though—how scared and worried we all were. So instead we just avoided any eye contact. We looked everywhere but at one another, waiting for the weird awkwardness of the moment to pass.

That was when a clap of thunder rattled the house to its foundations.

Everyone screamed.

∿∿∿

JOSIE

I had to veto Val's suggestion that we get tattoos. I tried to blame it on the multiple heart attacks my mother would surely have if I did that and she found out. But the truth was, I was relieved to have an excuse to pass.

"There's a difference," I told her, "between temporarily scribbling on the wall of a dive bar and permanently inking your body."

We cruised down Main Street, back in the direction of Riverdale. "Besides, we don't need ink to prove to everyone that we're fierce. They'd already know that—even if we hadn't tagged Venom's lair."

"I'm glad we did it, though," Val said. "It was fun."

"It *was* fun," I said, glad we were all in agreement. "And it had to be done. We've got turf to protect. We can't let anyone encroach on that."

"Speaking of which . . ." We pulled smoothly up to the intersection at a red light when I noticed something—the silver convertible in the next lane. "Mantle?" *Ignore the devil's incessant texts, and he shall appear . . .*

His eyes lit up when he saw me. He had another Bulldog riding shotgun, one I didn't know—please, I can't be expected to keep up with all my adoring fans. "Josie, how'd you know I was just thinking about you?"

"Mantle, be real—you're always thinking about me." He was only human, after all.

He didn't deny it. "Think your kitties can handle a race with the Bulldogs?" His seatmate *woofe*d at us, deep and guttural.

I glanced at my girls, but I didn't really have to. I knew what they were thinking. Why the hell not? We were all on a serious adrenaline rush and there was no reason to cut it short.

"You're on, Reggie," I said. "Tonight, the Pussycats grab back."

"I love a challenge," Reggie said. "Too bad this is gonna be E to the Z."

"We'll see about that."

The light changed red to green.

I revved my engine.

We flew.

CHAPTER NINETEEN

JOSIE

We squealed down Main Street, neck and neck. I didn't dare take my eyes off the road, but I could see Mantle in my side view. He was hunched over his wheel, gripping it, and his jaw was clenched. Brother was in it to win it. Too bad he'd crossed claws with the wrong cats.

The smell of burning rubber filled the air, and the girls shrieked with delight. We howled as I floored the pedal, edging out in front of Reggie. It was only a few inches— there went the mayor's office, a blur in our rearview mirror— but it was enough.

"CRAP!" It was Val. She was up and hanging over her door, eyes on the Bulldogs.

"What?" I pumped the brakes as softly as I could manage. Reggie in the mirror slammed on his brakes so hard the car fishtailed off into the opposite lane. I heard the boys curse, loudly. As they straightened out, I saw a figure step out past their car, crossing the road against traffic—our traffic— completely obliviously.

"Dilton Doiley?" Melody sounded surprised. "What the hell is he doing, randomly wandering Main Street in the dead of night?"

"I don't know, but he'd better snap out of whatever alternate reality zone he's in or he's gonna be roadkill," I said.

"Is this a sign for us, maybe? Time to pack it in and get home?" Melody sighed. "Just when tonight was getting interesting."

I watched, our motor running, as Reggie jumped out of his car and checked on Dilton. Whatever reason he had for skulking around the streets of Riverdale well past bedtime—a bold move in this town, props to my man—it was none of my business, and he was obviously fine. I honked the horn twice, quickly, and waved at Reggie. He looked up and gave me a quick wave of his own.

"Okay, kittens," I said, stifling a yawn. "It's been a night. Time for bed?"

∿∿∿

Cheryl:

Dear Cousin, would that I didn't have to disturb you on one of our last summer Saturday nights, but TeeTee is simply beside herself from these cryptic texts she's gotten from Sweet Pea.

Cheryl:

A flurry of ominous comments, followed by total ghostage. She's worried it's something big . . . which, naturally, had me thinking: Lodge? The only thing possibly bigger in our town would be MY Daddy Dearest—or yours—and they're off the menu right now.

Cheryl:

I don't know what, if anything, is afoot, but do keep your wits about you, and tell your beau to be sure to take any calls from his snake brethren.

∿∿∧

Josie:

I know I said maybe meet up, but the cats and I just almost ran down Dilton Doiley on Main Street. No idea where he's going by himself, at this hour, but he ALMOST didn't get there. My girls and I are ready to call this night. Meet me backstage after the Venom show tomorrow?

Sweet Pea:

Yeah, sounds good.

Sweet Pea:

Wait, you saw Dilton on Main? Just, like, walking alone?

Yeah, why?

Sweet Pea:

Nothing. Just . . . that's weird. He's okay, though?

Josie:

It was definitely at least ten kinds of weird. But yes, he's okay. So it's over, and I need my beauty sleep. TTYL

Sweet Pea:

TTYL

⌒⌒⌒

Sweet Pea:

Looks like PP got what she needed.

FP:

And she didn't have to go through us.

Sweet Pea:

Not directly, anyway.

FP:

Just keep quiet. If it's done, the Serpents have nothing to worry about.

I know. But what exactly is "done"?

Better we don't know, son. Don't ask questions you don't really want the answers to.

∧∧∧

BETTY

Dear Diary:

Final Girl. Was that me?

Going by the Black Hood story, sure. The name fit me to a tee. I was close to the killer, in contact with him the whole time, even while he was working to thwart me and simultaneously taking down people in my life, my world. People I cared about. In the end, it turned out the Black Hood was someone closer to me than I'd ever have thought possible.

Real horror movie fodder, definitely.

My phone buzzed in my pocket, sending little vibrations through me. I listened to Jughead describe the "rules" of horror movies. It made my skin crawl. This jokey little list was way too close to home.

If I took my phone out of my pocket, would I see more UNKNOWN calls on the log? Or would it be something "innocent"—just another text from my sister or mother, begging me to come home and join them for a cup of tea with their friendly neighborhood cult leader?

I <u>was</u> the Final Girl. The ultimate Final Girl. Otherwise, there was no explanation for the regularly occurring events of my life.

I didn't want things to be <u>normal</u>, necessarily—I never felt more alive, more myself than when Jug and I were on the trail of a case—but did everything have to be literal, actual life and death all the time? Weren't there fewer potentially fatal mysteries to unravel?

It was me. It had to be. I was the common denominator. Therefore, I was somehow causing the darkness that always found me, found my life and my circle. I was basically a magnet for it.

"Earth to Betty—" I heard it, but like it was from underwater or far away. It was Archie's voice, calling me, but I couldn't find the energy to reach back.

A violent clap of thunder, so loud all the dishes on the table jumped, jolted me back to reality.

We all screamed. The lights flickered. Once they were back on, though, soft and dim for deep night, but still illuminated, I could feel an embarrassed flush creep up my cheeks. I could tell my friends were feeling equally silly.

"That was…bracing," Jughead said. "A storm. Just what we needed, out here in the woods, to really cement the cliché. We can go from <u>Cabin in the Woods</u> to <u>The Fog</u>. There's a reason Carpenter's films are considered classics."

"Okay, without encouraging any further pathetic fallacy, or divine intervention—whatever device we want to ascribe our sudden 'dark and stormy night' to," Veronica said. She took a sip of her wine—but a small one, I noticed. And she had one arm reaching for the tiny espresso cup at her side, too. She obviously couldn't quite decide which mood she wanted to cultivate. I didn't blame her. "What do we know? That's where we left off, before we decided to go down a meta-horror rabbit hole."

"I have…one thing." Archie sounded very uncertain. We all looked at him. He pulled something from his pocket—a folded square.

"A note, Arch? From who?" I asked. The back of my neck tingled. It couldn't be anyone we <u>wanted</u> to hear from. I remembered the creepy, ransom-note-style letters I used to get from the Black Hood.

<u>My father.</u>

Archie shrugged, his face coloring. "I don't know. Not—not a friend, I don't think." He unfolded it, read it to us. "'<u>I know what you did.</u>' Big letters. Handwriting—but I don't recognize it." I beckoned for it, and he reluctantly passed it around the table.

"Oh," Jughead said, his voice smaller than usual. "A different movie. <u>I Know What You Did Last Summer.</u>" He tried to play it off. "The sequel was lame."

"What the…?" My voice trailed off as I took it in: the harsh lines, the crumpled paper. The frayed edges. My thigh jittered, like my phone was buzzing again, but when I reached for it, it was still in my pocket. My throat felt tight. "Guys, what's going on?"

"It was under my pillow. Upstairs," Archie said. "I have no idea who left it. There are no other clues. I mean, maybe the birds. Maybe that counts. What if they're connected?"

There was at least one other clue that I could think of. That damning ringtone, "Lollipop," when I'd been in the bathroom. I pulled my phone out, scrolled through the call log yet again.

Empty. No unknown callers.

Was it a clue? Were the pills messing with me? Or was I just straight up out of my mind?

I couldn't tell the rest of them about this.

Luckily, I didn't have to. Veronica spoke up first. "Not the only clue," she said, somber. "Or at least, I don't think so. When I was downstairs in the wine cellar, I checked the security cameras. Remember, like I'd planned to when we first got here? Before…" She shuddered. "…Before our little welcome basket from some rando townie creep?"

"Not an image that's easy to forget." Jug spoke for all of us.

Veronica took a breath. "Well, I went into the security room, where the camera bank is. I had this idea that maybe there would be some, I don't know, lost footage or <u>something</u> from the night with—well, <u>the night</u>." She sighed. "Of course, there wasn't. There's no way Daddy would be so sloppy as to leave such glaring evidence behind. But I saw something else."

"What was it?" I asked, not sure I really wanted to know.

"One of the cameras. It was out."

"Let me guess. The one that <u>would</u> have been trained on the front entrance," Jug said, folding his arms over his chest.

"The one that would have told us who left those birds," I breathed. Now it wasn't just my leg vibrating with phantom energy, it was my whole body.

"Someone did that." Archie stated the obvious, wild-eyed. "Someone killed that camera so they could dump those birds, as a message to us. Possibly—probably—the same someone who left this note for me."

"Meaning, someone _is_ watching us. NO question." I took a sip from my soda. It was lukewarm and way too sweet, but I choked it down.

"Meaning someone could _still be in the house_," Jughead whispered, with a slightly wild look in his eyes.

"Okay, this situation just became about forty percent more critical," Veronica said. "And it was plenty dangerous before. So what next, guys?"

As if in answer, another clap of thunder crashed, this time making the overhead light fixture sway. We all screamed again, no longer embarrassed at all.

This time, it felt earned.

Next to me, Jughead grabbed my hand.

The chandelier swayed again, more threateningly now. The door to the front porch flew open, crashing against its frame. Driving rain slammed through the open doorway in relentless, intense sheets.

"We've got to close that," Veronica said, shouting to be heard over the storm swirling in and around us.

That was when the power went out.

The lights flickered, and I let out a full-on shriek, way past any form of self-consciousness, thinking only of self-preservation. I definitely wasn't the only one who did.

I couldn't see my friends' faces through the pitch-black, but everyone grabbed hands now, somehow finding one another in the absolute darkness.

Around us, the storm pounded and howled.

PART THREE: DEAD RINGERS

CHAPTER TWENTY

JUGHEAD

I could only think of one other time in my life when I'd experienced such absolute dark.

No, not when the power went out in the trailer park, though that did happen with alarming regularity.

I'm talking about the time Dilton Doiley dragged me into the caves beyond Fox Forest for an *I Am Legend* meets *Survivorman* camping trip, claiming the End of Days was upon us.

It was a test run, he told me. He was polishing his skills.

∧∧∧

I'd come to him after a presentation for Spanish class gone completely off the rails. Dilton had stood in front of the class and lectured about Baley's Comet and the coming of the blood moon—both portents of the apocalypse, he said. Dude seemed like he was in a seriously bad way, and I felt for him. It didn't hurt that this all went down pretty shortly after my mom had taken

Jellybean and headed to Toledo. I was raw, and more sympathetic than I might otherwise have been.

Reggie and his boys mocked Dilton mercilessly after class, and I felt for him then, too. I definitely knew what it was like to be the ongoing butt of their jokes. Also working in Dilton's favor: Betty, not yet one-half of #Bughead but still holding more influence over me than I probably would have admitted, telling me that she was worried about his mental state.

It was hard to argue.

"Fine," I told her. "I could use another survivalist fix. It's been a month since I watched *The Colony.*"

I found him by his locker, spouting something about fire and brimstone to a severely freaked-looking Ethel Muggs. I caught the words *fallout* and *bunker,* and watched her turn tail and flee. I didn't blame her.

I told him I believed him, about the comet and the other stuff, the danger around us. It wasn't even that much of a stretch. Jason Blossom was dead, Archie and I were basically estranged, and my family was falling apart. If this *wasn't* the End of Days, then I didn't know what the heck it was.

"I have a place we can go," Dilton promised. "It's small, but it's safe. It'll just be me and you. Bring only what you can't live without. And don't tell *anybody.*"

It probably wasn't exactly what he had in mind, but I brought my beloved collection of Ginsbergs. Only my very favorites—I'd sworn to Dilton I'd be space-conscious. They were paperbacks! (He wasn't impressed.)

"You really believe this is the end, don't you?" I asked. We were flopped on a ratty cot deep in the cave, and I was starting to sweat. "And also, sidebar: Where is your mom?" I thought about my own father, no doubt hunkered over a pool table at the Whyte Wyrm, definitely not thinking about impending doom, and probably not thinking about me, at all, and my heart began to race.

"She's out of town," Dilton said, short. "She's often out of town."

So far, the only thing Dilton had told me was that his dad taught him how to prepare for a trip like this when he was little, before he died. "Just a trial run," Dilton said. "Someday, I'll make something stronger." He secured a tarp from the mouth of the cave to the ground, so that suddenly we felt very . . . contained.

I blinked. "Feels . . . secure." Was it warm in here? And—maybe I wasn't the expert to ask about father-son bonding, but this wasn't exactly the typical activity . . . was it?

I checked my phone, planning to send Betty a text, and realized I wasn't getting any signal. "We're too deep in," Dilton said.

I panicked. I ran for the mouth of the cave, and he dove on me. There was a tussle. In the end, I managed to shake him off and get away. But not before he flipped all his lanterns off, plunging us into a dark more absolute than death. I realized afterward that he had infrared glasses, so it didn't bother him. For me, it felt like being entombed.

I raced outside, shouting half-hearted apologies for bailing over my shoulder to Dilton.

I never did tell anyone about that night in the cave. Dilton had said it was a trial run, and I shudder to think what his upgrade would look like, but in the end, I felt crappy enough for backing out of a promise I hadn't really meant to make in the first place. If I couldn't keep my oath to Dilton, at least I could try to keep my word.

~~~~~~

Up until now, the night in that cave had been the most primal, terrifying darkness I'd known.

Now, though, the rain pelting down sounded as loud as stones hitting the front porch—which was about as apocalyptic as anything else I could think of. Next to me, Betty clenched my hand so hard she left bruises and gave a blood-curdling shriek to rival any scream queen's best. The rest of us shouted, too.

I fumbled with my phone until I could switch on my flashlight. Around me, everyone's eyes were wide, their breath fast. Our hair whipped against our faces with the force of the wind from the storm.

I had to tell them—about the crown Veronica and I had seen, and what *I'd* seen, just after, when she'd left. That was evidence, too. That was probably a clue. And we needed as much of both as we could get.

But before I could open my mouth, another phone lit up, sending a glow over Veronica's dark features. She looked angry, determined. "Far be it from me to let *anything* rain on my so-called parade," she said. "Power outage? I'll pass. A woman's work is never done." She stood.

"Where—where are you going?" Betty asked, looking ever so slightly on the brink. I was loath to admit it, but I was definitely worried about her.

"We might need flashlights. And I definitely need to check on that generator," Veronica said. "It's working, I know it is, so I need to get it up and running."

"You're going back downstairs?" Archie looked really unhappy to hear this.

"Back to the basement," she confirmed. She tilted her head at him. "Don't look at me that way, Archie. *It's fine.* I just need to check what's going on down there. I promise—"

"Don't say it," said Betty, without a trace of kidding in her voice.

"I promise," Veronica insisted, *"I'll be right back."*

CHAPTER TWENTY-ONE

VERONICA

I'll be right back.

Normally, I'm not one for superstitions, but why had I chosen those words? I couldn't help but lament that decision as I made my way—carefully, hugging the wall like I was expecting a ghost or some other unpleasant surprise to leap out—down to the basement.

One foot. The other.

Left. Right.

I tried to time my breathing to my steps. I needed to get downstairs and get the generator on *fast*, before the panic mode was triggered, but my feet didn't seem to want to cooperate. From upstairs, I heard some more shouting, muffled and distant. It was impossible to completely ignore, but I tried to focus.

Down the stairs. *Dark.*

Through the hallway. *Darker.*

Into the security room. *Darkest.*

My phone flashlight, which always seemed way too bright in my bedroom at night, now felt as puny and insufficient as a lone match. I waved it around the room, finally landing on the generator.

Its power light was stuttering, blinking red. That meant it had somehow tripped. I needed to restart it. It had a breaker somewhere on its back. I just needed to figure out which switch it was . . .

I moved toward the generator—and tripped. *Of course.* My phone clattered out of my hand and the room went dark again, blacker even than it had been upstairs, though that didn't even seem possible.

"Crap," I said to no one.

My voice echoed against the walls.

Okay, no big, I told myself, trying to psych myself up. Much like superstitions, I also wasn't prone to the so-called creeps, as a rule . . . but then, there are exceptions to every rule.

Tonight felt exceptional in all the worst possible ways.

I crossed my fingers that I'd be able to trip the generator in the dark, on my own. And that once the lights came back, my phone would still be at least minimally functional.

I was groping along the sides of the cold metal box— accidentally probing all sorts of grates and sharp edges that may or may not have been primed to electrocute me right off the mortal coil, so that was delightful.

That was when I heard it.

Low, shallow, even breathing.

Like a whisper . . . or, more accurately, a hiss.

I froze. Held my own breath in the hopes that what I was hearing was just my own steady panic.

Shh. Shh. Shh.

No. It wasn't me.

Somewhere, in that small, enclosed space, I could hear someone else—or some*thing* else—breathing.

There was a scrabbling sound, skittering, like rats in an alleyway behind even the most posh New York City restaurants.

I swallowed, the sound roaring in my ears, my pulse screaming against my temples. *It's your imagination*, I insisted to myself, even though I didn't believe that at all. *Don't freak out, it's just your imagination, Ronnie, there's nothing down h—*

Fingers wrapped around my leg.

I screamed.

CHAPTER TWENTY-TWO

ARCHIE

I tried.

I tried hard, really hard, to keep it together after the lights went out that second time. I reminded myself that the gang was here, that we all needed to keep calm and work together, that Betty in particular seemed a little twitchy and I needed to be strong.

But once those lights went out, the pictures started.

It was a like a slideshow from my nightmares, from the inside of my head.

(Black hood green eyes dark woods gun knife sin crow)

It was too much. It was like every piece of violence, every moment of fear I'd had since Jason's death, was raining down, reminding me of how close the calls had all been, how lucky we were to be alive at all . . . how unlikely we were to stay on any kind of lucky streak.

Jason's father, shooting him point-blank.

The Black Hood, gun trained on my father.

The night of the riot, Fangs coming so close to dying.

The night of the riot, Jughead coming so close to dying.

Each image was another body blow, each thought another invisible gut punch for me to absorb, to endure.

And then, just like that, I couldn't endure any more.

"Everyone okay?" Jug was taking inventory. I heard Betty mumble some kind of reply, but it wasn't very convincing. I couldn't hear her all that well through the roar of my own blood rushing in my ears.

It was too much, all of it, swirling in my chest like a tornado. I pressed my hands to my forehead, begging the storm of emotion to stay locked inside, but it burst—I shouted, an anguished cry that took me a minute to recognize as coming from my own body.

Betty and Jug cried out to me; I heard it, but I wasn't acting on my own, not anymore. Now it was strictly autopilot. Still screaming, praying for the images to stop, I ran outside, toward the woods. I didn't know where I was going. Only that I had to get away. Outside, at least, the chaos of the storm matched how I was feeling inside.

Behind me, the door slammed shut, followed by a loud click. That meant something, I dimly realized, about me getting back into the house. But I wasn't worried about that right now.

The only thing I needed right now was to run.

CHAPTER TWENTY-THREE

BETTY

"Everyone ok?"

Jug was asking, and I tried to reply, but my brain didn't want to help my mouth make words. Somewhere nearby, Archie was screaming, a sound I'd never heard from him, not even when his dad was shot. I heard a bang, rushing footsteps—Archie running outside.

Jughead called after him, called to me, but I didn't reply. My heart was pounding, straining against my ribs, clawing its way up my throat. My phone was buzzing in my pocket, lighting me on fire, and I thought it must really, actually, be ringing now . . . but when I took it out, I saw that I wasn't getting any signal.

"Crap! No signal," I said. I had to see. I had to check. And there was only one way I could think to do that.

Archie had gone outside. I had no idea why. But if I followed him, if I ventured out beyond the immediate area of the house, maybe I could pick up some more cell service.

"I'm going, Jug," I said, or tried to say, and ran. I felt Jughead grab my arm, but I shook him off, determined, and slipped through the door just before it closed and the automatic lock slid into place.

You're locked out, I realized, but I also realized that, right then, I didn't care.

I ran, one foot in front of the other, feet sinking into huge, cold puddles of mud and long, wet branches scratching my cheeks, my arms, snagging my hair as I streaked through the night.

It felt like I was running for years, forever, legs burning and rain running into my eyes. My phone was tight in my hand and I knew without even looking that I wasn't getting a better signal, wouldn't get one, that there wasn't a better one to get out here, somehow.

I tripped.

I don't know if it was a branch or a rock or just my own blind panic, but I stumbled and went down hard, my hands leaving imprints in the dank, grainy mud.

And then a strong hand was grasping mine, helping me to my feet, hugging me tightly. I wiped my eyes with my forearm, which didn't do much to clear the rainwater out, and looked up into Archie's deep brown eyes.

"What are you doing?" he asked, sounding frenzied.

"I was . . ." I didn't know, honestly—now that he was holding me, it seemed crazy, running out into the storm this way, in the middle of a blackout, getting locked out of the house . . . Now all I could wonder was *What the hell was I thinking?*

Behind Archie, I saw a rickety shed. For gardening, or supplies, or who knew what else. (I sort of doubted Hermione Lodge did much gardening in the deep woods surrounding her lake house, but I could have been wrong.) Really, it looked, right now, more like a set straight out of *The Blair Witch Project*, which was the last thing I needed to be thinking about. For a second, I could have even sworn I saw a light shining inside. I opened my mouth to ask Archie about it, to direct his attention to it, but I didn't have a chance to say anything.

Suddenly, a cloth sack—*a hood?!*—was slipped over my head. I heard Archie struggling, then a thud, and Archie groaned.

Then everything went mercifully blank.

CHAPTER TWENTY-FOUR

JUGHEAD

Archie and Betty. They were gone. They'd vanished into the night, into the storm, while I was frozen, my mind a blur of static.

When the door banged shut behind Betty, my first impulse was to race out after her. I realized in that moment, though, that a real flashlight would be my best bet for finding her, and that was downstairs, where Veronica was working on the generator. Something else we'd need ASAP if we wanted to make it out of here at all, much less possibly find some of the evidence we'd come looking for.

It was a split-second decision, gut instinct alone. I dashed for the basement to get to Veronica. The faster we got the generator up and got ourselves some flashlights, the faster we could get out into the woods and find Archie and Betty.

I dove for the door and ran down the stairs as fast as I could without wiping out completely. Out of the corner of my eye, I saw a flash of something—*someone?*—moving toward the exit. But before I could figure out what it was, I heard the door swing shut behind me.

Then I heard it *lock*—the way it had earlier.

Which meant Veronica and I were shut in. At least until we got the power back.

"Veronica!" I bellowed, hands out, groping blindly in the air and twisting doorknobs as I passed them.

One opened into a space that felt large, just based on the echoes of my own movements, though still dark as everything else downstairs—like, secret-bunker dark.

But I heard something as I poked my head into that room. It sounded like . . . someone crying?

"Veronica?"

"Jughead! Oh thank god. Everything's in lockdown. And I swear to god, I know this sounds crazy, but I really think there's someone else down here."

I thought back to the flash I'd seen by the door. "I'd love to reassure you, but I'm not going to write off the possibility. Let's just concentrate on getting out of here. Is the generator near you?" I had no way of telling where Veronica's muffled voice was coming from in the echoes of the pitch-dark basement.

"Yes, but I dropped my phone—I think I broke it, clearly not a major emergency, but also not great—and I can't see a thing. I know I sound like the classic Upper East Side prima donna here, but I have no idea what to do with this thing."

I had to laugh, despite everything. "Don't worry. I can walk you through it. Even the fancy ones, they're all pretty much the same. We cycled through plenty in the trailer park. Growing up in squalor had to have at least one advantage. I knew I'd figure out what it was, sooner or later."

"I mean, I'm not happy about your family's misfortune, but let me just say that right now I am beyond grateful."

From her spot across the room, Veronica described the generator's blinking lights and all the ridges and edges she could make out.

"All right," I said once I had a pretty good sense of what we were dealing with. "There should be two switches—like light switches, or the ones in a circuit breaker box—" I paused. *Has Veronica ever seen a circuit breaker box?* Just how prima donna were we talking, here?

"If you're wondering whether I've ever reset a breaker, the answer is yes. I won't hold your doubt against you."

Busted. "Okay, what you need to do is turn both of those switches at the same time. Like the exact same time. Can you do that?"

"I think I can handle it." Now she sounded wry. I heard some muffled sounds, probably her feeling around for the switches, then a few false-start snaps.

"Okay, well, it was at great cost to my manicure, but . . ." I heard her take a deep breath, or maybe I felt it in my own lungs, even though that made no sense . . .

There was a sharp *snap*, and then I did hear Veronica exhale, loudly, and then a moment later, the lights were flickering and I was blinking like a mole or a bear that had just come out of hibernation. I was in an office, I realized slowly. Similar to Hiram Lodge's office upstairs . . . but another one.

Was this his *inner* inner sanctum? Had I actually, finally found it at last?

Across the room, I saw a small, slanted door, like it led to a closet. Veronica tripped out, only slightly worse for the wear.

"Jughead Jones," she said. "My hero."

CHAPTER TWENTY-FIVE

VERONICA

Would I have preferred to see my Archiekins, or my number one ride or die, Betty, upon stepping out of the suffocating crypt that was the security room in Lodge Lodge? Sure. But while Jughead and I may have been an unlikely duo—bound together mainly by our devotion to our respective significant others—when that door swung open to an actual, full, person-sized room, I was one hundred percent thrilled to see him.

Jughead looked equally relieved to see me, though I'm sure at least some of that had to do with the lights coming back on. I watched him scan the room, taking it in.

"Welcome to Daddy's secret hideout," I said, smiling. He grinned back. "And here you thought you'd gotten lucky stumbling on his office upstairs. Is it what you expected?"

He glanced at the bearskin rug and shrugged. "Pretty much. They're very similar."

"Yes. They're all of a theme. But the best dirt is kept down here, where even the safes have safes. Lock and key squared. Close to the cameras and all his supervillain toys."

"Except . . . I don't think *all* his toys are down here," Jughead said. He smiled mischievously.

I realized he was holding something. "What's that?"

"I found it upstairs, after you saw that crown on the window," he said. "It's not labeled, but it's a thumb drive. I was going to show you guys before, but then the power went out. I don't know what's on it, but it was locked in a lockbox inside his desk—so I'm thinking it's probably important, even though it was up there."

I must have looked stunned, because he smiled. "I'm Betty's boyfriend. You think I haven't learned a thing or two about lock picking from her?"

"I'm impressed," I said. "Especially because I bet you anything that thumb drive matches this case." I showed him. "And that keeping them separate was by design."

It was a plastic case, divided into space for nine different drives—but it only held eight. I had found it on the floor near the generator when the lights came back on. *Possibly left behind by our intruder?* I quickly shook off the memory and continued. "I'm guessing the numbers in this case correspond to the cameras set up around the property."

"And this is the drive with the footage from the front entrance. With the crows—and whoever left them there," Jughead surmised.

"I think so. Or at least, I'm hoping beyond hope. Let's get the others—we can watch it."

He frowned. "Right. No. I mean, yes to watching it," he said, seeing my confused expression, "but the others—Betty and Archie, they, uh . . . I don't know, I think they freaked out or something. First Archie ran out, then Betty took off after him. I only came down here because I figured our best bet at finding them in the woods was to get those flashlights you were talking about."

Archie had flipped and run off? My whole body went hot with rage. Daddy had driven him to this: this terror, this blind panic. And now he was out there—thunder crashed at just that instant, as if to punctuate the thought as it occurred to me—in this hideous storm, possibly hurt in addition to losing his mind.

Enough is enough.

I grabbed two heavy-duty flashlights from the closet. I handed one to Jughead. "I think you figured right."

"Veronica." He held the flashlight in his hands, feeling its heft. "You could knock someone unconscious with this."

"Well, I may not have been a Girl Scout," I said, smirking, "but I learned at a very young age the value of being prepared."

We headed out into the night.

CHAPTER TWENTY-SIX

ARCHIE

My head throbbed. I was nauseous. And I was *cold*. Shivering, my clothes still wet from running through the rain. But it wasn't raining anymore.

Or—wait, it *was*, but the rain was happening outside, not on me. I could hear it, bouncing off the roof, which meant that *I* was under a roof, even though the last thing I could remember, I'd been standing out in the woods, in the storm, with Betty.

So where was I now?

I groaned and blinked my eyes. They were covered, I realized, blindfolded or something.

"He's awake," someone said, and then there was heat as a body moved closer to me and leaned, doing something with the blindfold at the back of my head, twisting it in a way that made a spot on my skull throb, right at the base of my neck.

There. It was off.

"Archie!" I looked to my left, and there was Betty, her face streaked with dirt and rain, her hair and clothes wet, like mine. I tried to jump up, to reach for her, but my hands were tied.

"What the hell?"

"It's okay, Arch," she said.

"Are *you* okay?" The question was directed at me, and I looked up to see who had asked it. It was the girl, the twin from the General Store. Her brother was next to her. They were wearing matching olive windbreakers, and they were wet, too, but not sopping like Betty and me.

Not sopping . . . because they'd been watching us, waiting for their moment to grab us and drag us off—I looked around—into the old shed outside Lodge Lodge?

It must've been a hunting shed, once upon a time. It was bare-bones, slats of wood bowing from years of weather. There was a shelf or something built along the inner perimeter, maybe for gutting prey? The wood there was dark and mottled and suspiciously stained.

Prey. Right now, that was Betty and me. Involuntarily, I shuddered.

"It was you two!" I yelled, fury rising. "You've been following us all night!" The van. There *had* been a gray van, and it had been the twins, watching us, all along.

"No, Arch—listen to them," Betty pleaded.

"The van—Betty—" I protested.

"Think about it, Archie," she said. "We saw the van outside Greendale. But the twins were working at the General Store when we pulled in." She gave me a look. "I was suspicious, too, *believe me*. But I think they're telling the truth."

"We have," the girl said, quiet and a little bit contrite. "Been following you, I mean. But—not in that van you've been seeing. And not for the reasons you think." She took a deep breath, like she was planning to explain.

That was when the door burst open.

CHAPTER TWENTY-SEVEN

BETTY

The air in the shed was humid and tense, all of us waiting for the girl—Amelia, she said her name was—to explain what was going on. I'd had a brief explanation when Archie was out, but he was struggling against his restraints, desperate to hear it.

That was when we heard a huge crash—the door being thrown open, bringing all the frenzy of the storm with it. Amelia screamed. I grabbed Archie. We all watched the door, tense.

It was Jughead and Veronica.

"Archie!" Veronica saw his hands tied and ran to him. "What's going on?"

"Well, look at that," Jughead said, staying remarkably calm, all things considered. "It's like Chekhov's creepy murder twins. If you introduce them in the first act, they have to go off in the third."

"We're not *murder twins*," the boy, who'd said his name was Paul, cut in. "That's what we've been trying to tell you."

"Great," Veronica snapped. "And while you're at it, one more question: Why the hell is he tied up?" She was kneeling on the ground next to Archie, fumbling with the ropes at his wrists.

"And who knocked me out in the first place?" Archie demanded.

"That's my fault," Paul said, sheepish. "But I swear," he added quickly, "it wasn't on purpose. It wasn't the plan. You can ask her." He pointed at me.

Everyone looked at me, waiting. "It's true," I admitted. "I mean, I was blindfolded, so I didn't actually see it happen, but they grabbed us and dragged us to the shed. It all happened so fast, I was too stunned to fight back, but Archie, you struggled, and both of you slipped. Arch, you went over backward and landed on a rock. Hard. You went out."

"Okay, but why am I tied up?" he asked again.

"We were afraid," Amelia said. "We thought that when you came to you might freak out and attack us instead of listening."

"You thought right," Archie said, glowering.

"Just listen to them," Betty said.

"You have exactly ten seconds to convince me why I shouldn't call the cops on you," Veronica said.

"You wouldn't," Paul said, "because that would tip your father off to the fact that you're here, which he doesn't know, and I'm pretty sure you don't want him to know, either.

And the reason that I know this is because we're on the same side."

"We know all about you guys," Amelia said, "and what happened with Cassidy."

"Uh, yeah. We remember. You seemed . . . *furious* about that, back at the General Store," Jug said.

"We are," Amelia said. "But not at you guys. Not really, anyway." She looked guilty and apologetic. "I mean, yeah, we can get a little riled up. You *do* seem like typical spoiled city kids. No offense."

"None taken," Veronica said, dryly.

"But we know it was Hiram Lodge who was behind Cassidy's murder. And that, most likely, he framed you." She looked at Archie. "Which is how we knew that whatever your reasons for being up here tonight were, they were probably going to get you in trouble with him—or worse."

"So you . . ." Veronica started, obviously confused.

"Well, it's a small community, Shadow Lake. Even smaller once you filter out the richies and focus on the old-time townies. Mr. Lodge heard that you guys were coming up here."

"*How?*" Jughead asked. Then he frowned, realizing. "We were talking about it in the diner . . ." He sighed. "Ben. I guess we shouldn't have just assumed he was in his own freaky little RPG world."

Amelia shrugged. "Mr. Lodge has eyes and ears every-where. So he heard—from whoever it was—and sent some of his goons to watch you. And, I guess, mess with you? *That's* what we were watching. Honestly—when we realized what was going on, we . . . well, I know you won't believe me, but we were going to warn you. To let you know what was going on. I know you must be freaked out. I'm sorry."

"Daddy *sent someone after us.*" Veronica folded her arms over her chest. "And then *you guys* went after them. This is twisted, even by Lodge standards. Beyond anything I ever dared allow myself to imagine."

"The birds," I said. Veronica's *father* had been behind the murder of murdered birds. Did that make it scarier than if it had been a stranger? I decided it did. Like learning that your father is the Black Hood—the realization that, to coin a phrase, the call is *actually*, definitely, coming from inside the house.

Or more specifically, from inside your own bloodline. Your own *family*.

"We got to the house too late to see who'd done that," Paul said.

"And that note, Arch," I said, realizing. "Whoever left it . . . they could have been *there with us, inside the house . . . the whole time.*"

Veronica's eyes went wide. "That means . . . that breath-ing I heard in the basement?"

"Might not have been your imagination," Jughead said.

Everyone took a moment to let that sink in. Under the circumstances, bedraggled and trapped in a creepy shed with a set of weird twins was actually the best possible outcome, considering.

"Okay, putting aside that truly chilling revelation, if all of Shadow Lake is in Hiram's pocket . . . why are you two supposedly on our side?" Jughead asked, cocking his head with suspicion.

Both twins' whole bodies tensed. "It's complicated. But . . . Well, our mother died. She was hit by a car three years ago," Amelia said.

I swallowed. "I'm so sorry."

Paul shrugged. "Yeah. The thing was, she was just crossing the street. Wrong place, wrong time. It was someone else's 'accident.' She was just collateral damage."

"It was a hit," Archie guessed.

Now it was Amelia's turn to shrug. "The person who *was* the target? Who also died? He'd been the president of the Shadow Lake Executive Board."

"And he'd just been fired, I dimly recall," Veronica said. "With extreme prejudice." Her eyes reddened. "Oh, Daddy. You do have a way with negotiations." She looked at the twins, her face full of sorrow and remorse. "I know there's nothing I can say, but I am so, so sorry." She shook her head. "Frankly, I'm surprised you don't hate us more than you do."

"It wasn't you. We know that. I mean, it's part of why Cassidy fixated on your house in the first place. But it wasn't *only* because you're a richie, and an out-of-towner. It was . . . well, it was at least a little bit personal. We told him not to. Especially with what we all knew about your father. He had to have had some idea what he was getting into." Amelia wiped at her own eyes now.

"You think you know," I said, relating all too well, "but when it comes to your own life, your own personal safety, it's hard to imagine . . ."

"Wasn't hard for us," Amelia said, her voice clipped and angry. "We saw it with our mom. Even though it was never proven."

"Hell," Paul said. "It was never even investigated."

"Of course it wasn't," Veronica said. "I'm sure Daddy has the local law enforcement paid off here, as well. How else would they have these bogus so-called witnesses against Archie?" She squared her shoulders. "Well, the good news is, at long last, we have at least *one* solid lead. We have a video. Jughead and I found it in the basement. Whoever it was that I heard scurrying around down there must have been looking for it, too. Their loss. It's security footage, we presume of those crows being left. Whomever we find on that video will have some answers for us."

Jughead pulled the drive triumphantly from his jacket pocket. "It's right—"

Just then, thunder clapped, so loud it rattled the walls of the rickety shed. Jughead jumped involuntarily and dropped the drive. It skittered across the shed, into a dark, dusty corner.

He looked at me, panicked. "Crap."

"Relax, Jug," I said. "It's going to be fine."

Paul was closest, and he bent down to retrieve our best hope for Archie's innocence. Suddenly, Paul hissed sharply. I turned to him and saw his eyes sharpen, alert. "Guys. It's most definitely not fine."

CHAPTER TWENTY-EIGHT

JUGHEAD

I turned to see what Paul was looking at. It was . . . a blinking red light?

My brain processed it on some lizard level before the rest of me caught up. I scrambled to my feet and reached to help the others up. *"OUT! NOW!"*

Once everyone was standing, I launched myself at the group, shoving them all out the door.

"Herc! Get down!" I pulled everyone behind a shelf of rock outcropping and pushed them low to the ground.

"What—" Archie started. But he didn't have a chance to finish the thought.

The next thing we knew, there was a near-sonic *BOOM*, so loud it made the thunder seem positively quiet by comparison. I could smell smoke, thick and pungent—even through the rain.

The shed was gone. Blown to bits.

Along with the only shred of evidence we'd found.

CHAPTER TWENTY-NINE

VERONICA

One minute, Paul was reaching for the flash drive. The next, everyone was shouting and Jughead had shoved us all outside, back into the rain. Archie had thrown himself on top of me, knocking me to the ground. Betty shrieked and I heard a huge explosion. And then there was only the roar of flames crackling and the smell of smoke, acrid in the air.

One by one, we stood. Coughing, blinking, easing ourselves out of the dirt one at a time, watching in utter disbelief as the shed burned nearby.

"That was . . ." Betty started.

"Our only piece of evidence," I confirmed. Tears sprung to my eyes. I wrestled against Archie's protective bear hug. "We have to get it!"

"Veronica! Stop!" He held tight. "It's over."

"It can't be over." Now I was crying in earnest, hot tears streaking my face.

"It is," he insisted.

But it wasn't. Not by a long shot. Because I knew, then, I was going to do whatever it took to protect Archie from my father.

No matter the cost.

CHAPTER THIRTY

BETTY

"It can't be over." That's what Veronica said, through thick sobs.

Even though I hadn't even known about the evidence she and Jug found until seconds ago, I knew exactly what she meant. My stomach sank and my head swam. I reached for my pocket, for the pill bottle—and then I remembered.

The bathroom. And the pills. I still didn't know if I had even taken them at all. My mind was filled with static, and my phone screen—still cracked, webbing spreading like disease—still said NO MISSED CALLS.

I took deep breaths, but the smoke in the air made me cough. Jug patted my back.

"Take it easy," he said. "You don't want to breathe this in. It's not good for you."

I shoved my hands into my pockets and tried to make myself smaller, for him. For my friends. Tried to pull myself together for what felt like the millionth time in just the last few hours.

I was broken. Falling apart. I'd known it since before I was sure, before it'd been revealed with absolute certainty, that my father was the Black Hood. And I didn't know how the hell to get better. Not the Farm (god, no). Not the pills, either—though I wasn't going to give them up, not yet.

I wasn't ready to talk to Jug about it all, to be totally honest. It wasn't that I thought he'd judge me, I knew he'd be nothing but loving and supportive . . . It was that *I* was judging *myself.* I felt awful about the spiral I was in. And I was too ashamed to talk about it.

"You guys," I said, forcing myself to focus on the problem right in front of us: the shed, engulfed in flames, throwing heat in our direction.

"You guys, what are we going to do?"

CHAPTER THIRTY-ONE

ARCHIE

"You guys, what are we going to do?"

It was Betty. Her voice shook.

The shed was gone. The surrounding brush was smoldering. The air smelled like smoke and wet earth. And every time I closed my eyes, I saw Andre hovering over Cassidy, fierce and decided.

I know what you did.

"There's nothing to do, guys." My voice was strong, clear. It didn't give away any of the nerves running through me. Because this one thing, at least, I was sure of.

"We tried," I said. "We took our last shot, and . . . I don't know, maybe we almost found something. *Maybe.*"

"But Archie, that footage—" Veronica said.

"We never got a chance to watch it," I pointed out. "We don't *know* what was on it. Not really. And, come on—if your father can arrange *this*"—I nodded at the flaming wreckage—"then we're kidding ourselves to think we could get the best of him."

"Don't you dare give up, Archie Andrews," Veronica said, looking furious.

I shrugged. "Ronnie, this thing with your dad? It's looking more like a war than a battle. *This* was a battle. And we lost it."

"We can't give up!" Betty said. She was crying now, too.

I looked at them, at their open, searching faces. I hated what I was putting them through, hated how going home now made it all even worse. But what else was there to do?

"Guys, the verdict comes in next week," I reminded everyone. "We need to go home, to prepare."

Jughead cleared his throat. "He's not wrong." At the girls' incredulous looks he clarified. "I mean, I don't think we should give up—I'm definitely not suggesting that. But we *should* get out of here. There was an explosion. Soon there'll be cops. We need to not be here when they arrive."

It was hard to argue with that.

"We should report the fire. Before someone else does." Betty seemed to snap back into problem-solving mode. "At least control one tiny part of the story for as long as we can."

I nodded, along with all the others. But I couldn't help but laugh about it, bitterly, to myself:

It was ridiculous, pretending any part of this was in our control.

EPILOGUE

Ethel:

Dilton, I'm worried about you. I know you said you couldn't meet, but could you at least text me back? Let me know everything's OK? Maybe I'm being paranoid, but I can't shake the idea that something's going on.

Dilton:

It's done.

PP:

Good news. Payment will be dropped in the location we discussed by 5 a.m. tomorrow. I wouldn't wait on picking it up if I were you.

Well, what do you know? The boy came through. Though if I were you, I'd maybe wonder about what kind of high school kid has those sorts of explosives just lying around.

HL:

Your concern is duly noted. I appreciate your cooperation in all this. Your people will receive compensation.

PP:

Anytime. I scratch your back . . .

HL:

You wait, until the next time I need a back-scratching. That's how this works.

PP:

Understood.

∿∿∿

PP:

You'll be thrilled to hear that your man Doiley hooked us up.

Sweet Pea:

Happy to be of service. But I told you, I'm out of this. I found Dilton for you, now I'm done.

PP:

When will you learn? There's no such thing as "done." There's only "in" or "dead." And for now, you're "in." That means you're on Hiram Lodge's good side. You probably want to keep it that way.

∧∧∧

JUGHEAD

In the end, we decided an anonymous phone call was the only way to report the fire. Not that we really needed to call it in at all; chances were, Hiram Lodge had already warned the police that there was going to be some kind of explosion up at the house.

Or, hell—maybe it was the police that he'd paid to blow the shed up in the first place.

The thing was, we'd never know the truth. Shadow Lake was already buried too deep under the long arm of Hiram Lodge. That anyone out there was on our side, was trying to help us gain even the tiniest foothold in the name of justice, was amazing enough in itself. We couldn't expect anything more. Couldn't dare hope.

But we did, somehow. Hold out hope, against all odds.

Hope that Veronica's father still retained even a semblance of humanity, of empathy and love for his daughter and those who populated her world.

Hope that even as our video evidence burned, there was something else—some note, some message, some hidden object that would unravel this whole sordid mess—something out there that we would surely find, if only we searched *just a little harder.*

Hope that Archie would go free.

Hope springs eternal. That's the expression, after all. But spring had come and gone, and with it, the possibility of a golden rebirth. Instead, we were left with the unrelenting fire of the last days of summer, blazing a bright, hot path straight to Labor Day, straight to the courtroom . . .

And straight to the end of Archie Andrews's lingering innocence.

ABOUT THE AUTHOR

© JDZ Photography

Micol Ostow has written over fifty works for readers of all ages, including projects based on properties like *Buffy the Vampire Slayer, Charmed*, and most recently, *Mean Girls: A Novel.* As a child, she drew her own Archie Comics panels, and in her former life as an editor she published the *Betty & Veronica Mad Libs* game. She lives in Brooklyn with her husband and two daughters, who are also way too pop culture–obsessed. Visit her online at micolostow.com.